THE HONEYMOON THAT WASN'T

BY
DEBBI RAWLINS

MILLS & BOON®

First published in Great Britain 2007
by Harlequin Mills & Boon Limited, Eton House,
18-24 Paradise Road,
Richmond, Surrey TW9 1SR

© Debbie Quattrone 2006

ISBN: 978 0 263 85578 4

14-0607

Printed and bound in Spain
by Litografia Rosés S.A., Barcelona

DEBBI RAWLINS

Even after swearing she'd never move again,
Debbi Rawlins recently relocated to central Utah
with her husband, Karl, where she adopted Dugly,
a half tabby-half Siamese cat, and a puppy named
Maile. When she's not writing she can be found
feeding apples to the deer, who are too numerous
to name. So she calls them all Piggy.

This is for Logan,
the newest addition to our extended family.
The cutest baby in the world.

Prologue

To: The Gang at Eve's Apple
From: LegallyNuts@EvesApple.com
Subject: Insanity

I'm not sure why I'm writing to you guys. Besides the fact that it's three in the morning and I can't sleep. I know the reason for the insomnia, which doesn't help one bit. Tomorrow night, no, <sigh> I guess technically tonight, is my sister's wedding rehearsal dinner. That part's great. She's met this terrific guy and I'm really happy for her.

The problem is that I'll see Tony again. A friend of my sister's. He's part of the wedding party. I met him only once, almost a year ago at the job site where they worked. He was wearing a tight white T-shirt and, my, oh, my, what a chest.

He's tall, too, at least six feet, broad shoulders, dark wavy hair, chocolate-brown eyes and a kind of square jaw. You get the picture. The guy is hot.

So why am I dreading tonight like I would a trip to the dentist? But I'm also looking forward to it. Does that make sense? If so, explain it to me, would you?

Oh, by the way, I'm not new to the group but I've been lurking for a while. To be honest, I never thought I'd post anything. Too busy. And besides, it's not my style. Or so I thought. This guy has my brain going in circles.

Frankly, if I were by myself and met him at a bar, it would be a no-brainer. I'm not into one-night stands though for him I'd make an exception. But that he knows my sister, and will be meeting my parents and brother tonight, complicates everything. I'm definitely not interested in anything long-term. Anyway, he's not someone who's in the game plan. No one is, really. I've been lucky. My career is taking off. A social life? What's that?

I'm a lawyer and due in court in six hours. I'm so tired. I truly wish I could sleep. But that's not going to happen. And now I'm rambling. Enough. If anyone is out there with some advice or even to confirm that I'm totally out of my mind, I'd appreciate it.

Thanks for reading this.

D

DAKOTA STARED at her laptop's screen for a moment. She was tempted to erase the e-mail. Writing it had been therapeutic—she didn't need to send it. Nor did she really need a reply. Nothing anyone could write would make her act on her impulse to spend a carte blanche night with Tony. She was too chicken to do anything like that. Not to mention that her family knew him. Or they would by tonight.

Her fingers hovered over the keyboard. What did she have to lose? If she were to get a response, at least it would be something to do since she couldn't sleep anyway. Besides, what would it hurt to get some feedback? She pressed the send button before she could change her mind again.

After setting the laptop on her nightstand, she got rid of one of the pillows she'd stacked behind her back and plumped the remaining one before sliding down, cradling her head in it and staring at the shadowy ceiling.

How totally bizarre was it to e-mail a bunch of women she didn't know—well, in a way she knew them. After hours and hours of reading their uncensored, heartfelt outpourings, she knew them, all right. Maybe even better than their friends and family.

Sheer genius had inspired the concept for the Eve's Apple Web site. Membership was simple. If there's a guy you're hot after you qualify. Not the right guy, in fact, more likely the one you absolutely wouldn't take home to Daddy. But he's also the guy you can't stop thinking about. You know you have to have him just so that life can get back on track. So that you could eventually settle down with Mr. Right and not have to wonder. Posting was like going to a twelve-step meeting. Anonymous so you could really vent, and everyone there really got it. They shared experiences, and gave advice when asked. Kind of like free therapy.

Odd how she could put it all out there for these strangers, but not talk to Dallas about Tony. Not that her sister would disapprove. On the contrary, she'd likely urge Dakota to go for it. But that was the difference between them. Dallas did whatever she wanted. Family expectations meant little to her. Not Dakota. Always the good girl, she'd even followed in her father's and brother's footsteps.

But it wasn't a sacrifice. She loved the law. In fact, she adored everything about her job. Dakota Shea for the defense, Your Honor—was her favorite expression. She wouldn't change any of it. Her social life, on the other hand, was a joke. If she could even call having a drink once every other week at the local lawyers' hangout a social life. Oh, and dinner at her parents' Tarrytown house one Saturday a month.

She closed her eyes, praying for sleep. When it wouldn't come, she tried thinking about work, mentally preparing herself for her court appearance in a few hours. But the distraction only lasted a few minutes before her thoughts drifted back to tonight. Back to Tony.

Groaning, she rolled over onto her side and grabbed the pillow she'd discarded. Comfortably sitting up again, she placed her laptop in front of her. She turned it on and saw she had a new e-mail. Good God, someone from Eve's Apple had already replied.

To: LegallyNuts@EvesApple.com
From: BabyBlu@EvesApple.com
Subject: Losing it
   Hey, D, just read your post. Yeah, I'm an insomniac, too. And we share another similar problem.

A guy. Go figure. While it's not too late for you though, I've already blown my chance.

You see, I was once exactly where you are. Worried about my career, worried about what my parents thought (I'm Jewish, he isn't), worried about having all the right accoutrements to my upwardly mobile life.

Dakota stopped reading. Similar problem? Where had this woman—Dakota glanced down at the name—Carson, gotten all this crap? Rather large assumption. Dakota hadn't mentioned anything of this nature. None of it applied. Not really. Okay, so maybe her parents were an issue, to the extent that they'd had a vision for her early on, encouraging her to study law and now strongly hoped that she'd eventually become a judge. Just a minor issue. It wasn't as if she allowed them to govern her life. Sure, she relished their approval but what child didn't?

As far as her career went, well, she was sufficiently secure. No worries there. Not that she wanted to test the waters… But that didn't mean she was anything like Carson.

Her gaze was drawn back to the e-mail. She couldn't help herself and resumed reading.

And to my parents' delight, I became wildly successful. Mainly thanks to the real estate boom, doncha know? Yep, I'm a realtor, commercial sales mostly—high end. And that's how I met Larry. He was a finish carpenter working on one of the buildings I was showing to a client.

Dakota abruptly stopped reading. A carpenter? That was creepy. Tony wasn't a carpenter but a construction worker. Close enough. Professional woman meets blue-collar guy. Sounded like one of those awful talk shows on television with everyone screaming at each other.

She shuddered. Fatigue was really doing a number on her imagination. She left the rest of the e-mail unread and then skimmed a couple more that had popped up, both encouraging her to go for it. Then she signed off. She needed sleep. Not just for her court appearance, but to get through this evening. Without making an ass out of herself.

1

"SHE'S GOING TO BE LATE."

Tony San Angelo looked at his friend Dallas. "Who?"

She smiled and sipped her martini. "Dakota's always late on Friday nights. Too much happening at the office."

"Hey, you're getting married. It's a big thing. She can't make it to her only sister's rehearsal dinner on time?"

"As long as she's not late to the church tomorrow, I don't care." She elbowed him. "Relax. She'll be here."

"Like I care."

"Uh-huh." Dallas took another sip, trying to hide her smile.

"Nice place," he said, pretending interest in the private dining room of the swank Manhattan restaurant. Hadn't Dallas already told him he had zero chance with her sister? Not that he believed that. "I hope you and Eric didn't have to spring for this little soiree."

"Eric insisted on it because my parents are paying for the wedding. My father did try to argue because

Eric's parents are gone. Yada, yada. You know how all that male posturing goes."

"What are you looking at me like that for?"

She grinned.

"Hey, I'm wounded."

"Kidding," she quipped. "You're the least macho guy I know."

"Ah, man. Now I'm irreparably wounded."

"Okay, I'll try this again. You're macho without the macho mind-set. Better?"

"Hey, hey, break it up. People are talking." Eric joined them and clapped Tony on the arm. "Good to see you."

"I wouldn't miss this. Our little Dallas getting married. Hope you plan on keeping her barefoot and pregnant."

She socked him in the arm.

Eric chuckled. "Now, now, children."

Tony liked him. Great guy for Dallas, even if he was a suit who worked off Madison Avenue.

A waiter came in, and said something to Dallas's father. He nodded and then called for everyone's attention, giving them a two-minute warning before dinner would be served.

The rest of the bridal party was already there, nibbling on shrimp and imported cheeses, and guzzling drinks, all the really premium stuff. Even Dallas's snobby brother had made it on time, and he was one of the head honchos at the law firm where Dakota worked.

Tony drained his beer, the trusty domestic kind,

and sat at the far end of the long, elegantly set table. The seat gave him an excellent view of the door, not that he was that anxious to see Dakota again. Okay, maybe he was. The woman was totally beautiful. Light brown hair, gray-blue eyes, incredible legs. But his strategy had more to do with keeping his distance from the senior Sheas.

Dallas's parents had been cordial enough, but that didn't mean he'd like to make small talk with them. They were different, too serious in his opinion; both scholars, he a judge, she a professor. Tony was strictly blue-collar. A college dropout. No regrets. He liked his no-headache job, liked living life on his own terms, not getting calls in the middle of the night like his pop did.

Nancy sat next to him. She was the only other person here he knew besides Dallas because they'd all worked on the same construction crew at one time.

At first he thought Nancy had bumped his knee by mistake when she scooted her chair closer to the table, but then she did it again. He looked over at her.

"Why do we have so many forks?" she murmured, her lips barely moving.

"Beats me. But I know you're supposed to work from the outside in."

"Okay." She dubiously glanced around at everyone else and, mimicking them, placed her white linen napkin on her lap.

"The hell with it, I'm eating with my fingers."

Her stricken gaze flew to him.

"That was a joke."

She gave him a reproachful look, and then smiled at the white-gloved waiter as he set her Caesar salad in front of her.

Tony sighed. That was the trouble with these high-class places. You couldn't relax. Have fun. Of course he'd keep his opinion to himself. He'd never hurt Dallas. This wasn't just her wedding—these were her people.

His attention strayed to the door. Still no Dakota. No one seemed concerned. Not even Mr. and Mrs. Shea. In fact, from what Dallas had told him, they probably approved that she put work ahead of everything else.

Man, he didn't understand these people. His parents would've given him or any of his three siblings a lecture right then and there. In front of everyone. The deal had always been, if the kids were willing to screw up in public, then they got reprimanded likewise. Even though none of them were kids anymore.

While being on time for a party in the San Angelo family was never a problem. When his older sister had gotten married the party had started two days before the wedding and didn't end until three the morning after the reception.

The salad plates were cleared and the rack of lamb was just being served when Dakota showed up. Still dressed in her navy-blue power suit, she had her hair pulled back in an awful, matronly style. Nancy and the other bridesmaid were all gussied up, Dallas more causally elegant in a simple cream-colored silk dress.

Dakota looked directly at him, and he smiled. Her gaze fluttered away and his smile broadened.

"I've never had lamb before," Nancy whispered. "Have you?"

"Yeah." He briefly glanced over to see her skeptically staring at her plate, and then his attention went right back to Dakota.

She took the vacant seat Dallas had saved next to her, and damned if Dakota didn't slide him another look.

"Tony?"

"What?"

Nancy made a face. "Are you listening to me?"

"What did you say?"

"I want to know what this green stuff is. It looks like jelly."

"It is. Mint jelly. It goes with the lamb."

"Right." Nancy snorted. "Come on. If you don't know just—what are you looking at?" Until Nancy followed his gaze, he hadn't realized he'd been staring. "Oh, Dakota's here." She waved excitedly, and Dakota waved back.

Only at Nancy. Not at him. Good sign.

He smiled, thinking about the first day they'd met. The *only* day they'd met. She'd appeared at the job site to see Dallas. It was love at first sight for him. Okay, more like lust. Dallas had noticed his interest. Told him to forget it. But the eye contact he'd made with Dakota told him otherwise. If it had lasted one second less, it would have been a different story. And when she got to the end of the block and turned around, he knew.

"How do you know her?" he asked Nancy.

"Well, duh. She's the one who helped us with all

our legal stuff to scare Capshaw into taking our harassment complaints seriously. For free, too."

Tony's gaze returned to Dakota. A woman full of surprises. He thought she'd be too busy to help a group of women fight discrimination against the state's second largest construction company.

"You haven't met her." Nancy leaned closer, eyeballing him with far too much interest. "Have you?"

"Why?"

"Have you?" She darted a look at Dakota, probably wondering why she hadn't acknowledged Tony. Nancy seemed to arrive at her own conclusion, judging by the smirk on her face as she settled back in her chair. "She shot you down."

"What?"

"There's actually a woman in this city who isn't gaga over you."

"Get out." He grabbed his beer and took a deep pull.

"Tell me you don't know that all the women at work are in heat over you."

"Yeah, right. Especially Jan."

Nancy rolled her eyes. "I meant the straight ones. So what happened?"

"I met her once for about forty seconds."

"You must be slipping." She grinned. "It usually takes only ten for women to start getting stupid over you."

"That how long it took you?"

Her grin disappeared and her cheeks got pink. He knew that would shut her up. What he didn't know was that he'd been the subject of gossip.

Shit.

Hadn't he been the only guy on the work crew who'd been willing to speak up on the women's behalf? Although most of the other guys were guilty of the harassment management chose to ignore. Still, he could've kept his mouth shut. But he hadn't. And now he wasn't working for Capshaw Construction anymore.

Fine by him. Being discussed by a bunch of chatty women wasn't.

Through the rest of dinner, he and Nancy didn't speak much.

She was busy choosing forks and eating, and he was busy trying not to stare at Dakota. The woman really needed to smile more. She looked too damn serious. The way she wore her hair pulled back didn't help.

All of a sudden, her gaze swept toward him, meeting his eyes dead-on. She locked into him for one long hypnotic moment, and then blinked and looked away.

Excitement thrummed through him. The awareness in her gray-blue eyes was like a vice around his neck, restricting air, making it hard to breathe. To say nothing of the effect she was having on him south of the border. The woman definitely had him by the balls. What did she intend to do with them?…was the question.

"DID MOTHER TALK to you about the photographer?" Dakota foolishly asked her sister, in a vain effort to keep her mind and eyes off Tony.

"No." Dallas frowned, immediately setting down her wineglass. "What about him?"

"Oh, nothing. I mean she wants to make sure the wedding party knows they don't have to stop at his studio before the reception."

"Right," Dallas said slowly, her frown deepening. "I knew that."

"Good. Just checking." Dakota gave her a weak smile and then finished off the rest of her chardonnay.

The corners of Dallas's mouth twitched and she glanced toward the far corner of the table. At Tony.

Damn.

Dakota clenched her teeth. Was she really that absurdly obvious? Probably. Her sister knew her better than anyone. Which also meant Dallas should understand that Tony was unquestionably the wrong kind of guy for her.

The thought struck like a bolt of lightning, coming from some dark void and stunning her. Shaming her. She glanced around worried that someone could read her ugly thoughts.

Her parents were chatting with Eric's friend Tom and his wife Serena, both of whom were in the wedding party. Nancy, a woman who'd worked with Dallas, and Dallas's roommate, Wendy, both sat on the other side of Eric.

And then there was Tony. Looking directly at her, his dark eyes sparkling in the mellow glow of the crystal chandelier. His lips curved slightly, and then he winked.

She lowered her gaze, removed the white linen napkin from her lap and brought it to her lips. Even though she'd yet to take a bite of her entree. The others were already being served dessert and coffee, and she could have easily skipped eating altogether except she didn't want to upset her mother.

Sighing, she picked up her fork and knife. At least while she ate she could politely ignore Tony. Dallas and Eric were tête-à-tête and Cody had vacated the seat to Dakota's left five minutes ago to make a phone call. Not that she had much to say to him. Being with her brother at the office for twelve hours a day was quite enough.

She slid a glance toward Tony. The chair next to Nancy was empty. Dakota jumped at the hand on her shoulder and swung her gaze around.

Tony grinned, his teeth brilliantly white against his tanned face. "Dakota, right? Dallas's sister?"

"Yes, we've met once before, haven't we?"

The corners of his mouth quirked up slightly and he gestured to Cody's vacant chair. "You mind?"

"Suit yourself." She cringed at the defensive lilt to her voice.

He didn't seem to notice, just lowered himself into the chair, mindless of the way his thigh brushed hers. How when he angled toward her, his knee touched her knee. When he stretched his arm along the back of her chair and leaned close, her heart nearly exploded through her chest.

"I have a question."

"Yes?" She inched back to look at him without coming nose to nose. Bad enough his warm sweet breath managed to caress her chin. God, he had such thick dark lashes. So not fair. And his smile as he got closer…

"It's kind of personal."

She swallowed. What could he possibly—

"Ah, Tony." Dallas leaned over. "Glad you decided to slum it."

"Right." They exchanged the look of longtime friends.

"You remember Dakota," Dallas said, the impish gleam in her eyes all too familiar.

"Yeah, we were just getting reacquainted until you butted in."

Dallas laughed. "So charming, isn't he?" She glanced briefly at Dakota and then turned a more serious expression toward Tony. "I need to talk to you before you disappear tonight."

"Disappear?" He grinned at Dakota. "My motor is just getting revved."

She tried to keep a straight face. Tried not to look around to see if anyone heard. Especially not her mother. She picked the napkin off her lap again and pushed back her chair. "Excuse me, please. I have to make a phone call."

"Something I said?" Tony asked, his amused dark eyes watching her rise, lingering briefly on her breasts. Not long enough to be rude, but long enough to make her feel as if she were twelve again, awkward, nervous and wanting to suddenly disappear rather than face her parents' reaction, her mother's accusing eyes because Dakota had put herself on display.

She dropped the napkin over her plate and pushed in her chair.

"Aren't you going to finish your dinner?" Tony couldn't quite keep his amusement in check. "No dessert unless you clean your plate."

She ignored him and addressed Dallas. "You two go ahead and have your talk."

"Come on, Dakota. You just got here. Besides, I need to talk to you, too." Dallas gave her a pleading look that almost had her caving. After all, tomorrow was Dallas's big day....

As hard as it was to say no to her sister, Dakota shook her head and picked up her briefcase. Tony was headed someplace she didn't want to go. At least not here. Certainly not with an audience. "I'm leaving."

"I'll have them bring your bananas Foster."

"Think I'll pass." In spite of herself, Dakota glanced at Tony.

"Hmm, that's what you call that stuff. Some guy named Foster must have come up with it, huh?"

Dallas laughed.

Dakota couldn't tell if he was kidding or not.

"They're supposed to offer cognac and then we're done here," Dallas said, looking over her shoulder at the headwaiter, who'd already brought out the bottles of brandy. "So if you can't stay—"

"What?" Tony spread his hands. "No dancing?"

"Down, boy. That's tomorrow night," Dallas quipped. "As if you can dance."

"You talkin' to me?" Tony scoffed. "Do you have any idea who taught Travolta his moves for *Saturday Night Fever*?"

"What were you, about three?"

He shrugged, a grin curving his mouth. "I'm just saying…"

Dakota shook her head, a little envious of their easy camaraderie. "As I said, I'm leaving."

Tony stuck out his chin in acknowledgment. "See ya tomorrow."

"Right." Everyone at the table seemed preoccupied so she skipped a farewell and headed for the door.

"Don't be late," he added.

Dallas half groaned, half laughed.

Annoyed, Dakota stopped, but then thought better of turning around and calling attention to them. She kept walking, wondering how in the hell she'd ever found this man attractive.

WATCHING HER SISTER walk out in that ramrod straight   I'd-better-get-out-of-here-before-I-kill-somebody posture Dallas knew too well, she sighed. "Why do you have to antagonize her?"

Tony dragged his gaze away from the empty doorway. "I think she likes me."

"You're impossible."

He smiled. "A little wine, a little tango tomorrow night…" He flattened a hand to his belly and made a swaying dance move. "She'll be ripe for the picking."

"Excuse me? We're talking about my sister here."

"Hey, I'm just talking about asking her out. Where's your mind at?"

She gave him a mock glare. Tony was a great guy. Perfect for Dakota if she'd give him a chance. But she wouldn't. Too many expectations blocked the way. Father wanted her to be a judge, and Cody, a senior partner at the law firm where Dakota worked, not only expected her to rake in the dough but attract high-end clients. Mother, well, she always expected too much of everyone.

"Seriously, Tony, I need a favor."

"Shoot."

She glanced over at Eric's friend to be sure he wasn't listening, and then leaned closer to Tony. "Remember how I met Eric. Through a prank his friend Tom pulled?"

"Yeah."

"We think he's up to something again. Like sabotaging our honeymoon."

"No way." Tony gave Tom a harsh look. "Not your honeymoon."

"You don't know Tom. He lives to create the perfect practical joke."

"Want me to talk to him?"

"No, no. I don't even want him to know we suspect anything. What I would like you to do is act as a decoy." Dallas felt Eric stirring behind her. Obviously he'd heard, or at least knew what she was doing. They'd discussed the ploy. He didn't agree with her interference. But of course he didn't understand the complexities of growing up a Shea.

"Decoy? How?"

"You can take a long weekend, right?"

"Uh, yeah," he said slowly.

"Ever been to Bermuda?"

Tony frowned in disbelief. "You're not saying—you're kidding."

"The plane leaves right after the reception. The hotel is already booked and paid for."

"Do you know how crazy this is?"

Eric's cheek touched hers as he leaned close enough for them to hear. "That's what I told her."

She elbowed him. "Be quiet."

"Just tell him you're going to Hawaii." Tony chuckled.

"He heard Eric making the arrangements but he doesn't know that we decided to go on a cruise instead. I want to keep it that way."

"This still sounds crazy. It's not like he's gonna follow you to Bermuda."

"Have I ever asked you for anything?"

"Wow, Dallas, go ahead and turn the screws, why don't you?"

"It's a free vacation, for goodness' sake."

"You realize there's one huge hole in this plan," Tony said, giving Eric that smug condescending male look she hated. "Don't *two* people normally go on a honeymoon?"

It was her turn to look smug. "Of course. That's why Dakota will be going with you."

Hell, why didn't she say that in the first place?

2

"I NOW PRONOUNCE YOU man and wife."

Tony watched Dallas and Eric embrace, and then looked at Dakota. Her eyes were glassy, blinking rapidly, and her smile quivered slightly as she gazed at her sister.

Today was the first time he'd seen her with her hair down, longer than he'd expected, hanging just below her shoulders, light brown and full of honey-colored highlights. And really shiny. Outside he'd caught a glimpse of her entering the chapel, her hair a brilliant silky mass floating around her shoulders.

He was one of those suckers for women with long hair and Dakota was way up there on the perfect scale. His groin tightened, thinking about tomorrow, Dakota, a sunny beach, a skimpy bikini and all that hair.

Assuming she'd agreed to the plan. Dallas was supposed to have talked to her this morning. Him, he already had a small bag packed, waiting in his car to be transferred to the limo. Dallas didn't think there'd be a problem with Dakota, only that she might not want to stay the whole weekend. Just turn around and come back to Manhattan tonight. That's where he'd have some convincing to do.

She looked over at him just then and he smiled. Her lips curved ever so slightly. Ah, progress. But she gave up eye contact, her gaze going back to her sister as the cello music started, signaling them to leave the altar and start down the aisle. Dallas and Eric went first and then everyone else in the wedding party followed in no particular order. The men wore tuxedos and the women long dresses. The way Dakota filled out the dark red dress made it hard to keep his eyes on Dallas and Eric. The neckline wasn't too low but it showed off a tempting amount of pale satiny skin and a hint of cleavage. He was lucky enough to walk behind her, or maybe unlucky, because the gentle sway of her hips and the way the dress cupped her curvy backside got a reaction from him that he had trouble hiding.

They got outside and pews of friends and family followed, hugging, kissing cheeks, shaking hands, but not a single grain of rice was thrown. Probably not a custom at high-class weddings. When his sister had gotten married, his pop distributed a whole twenty-pound bag of rice. Made a special trip to Chinatown to get it.

"Okay, everyone." After the initial commotion, the photographer motioned the wedding party to stand in front of one of the large stained-glass windows.

The Union Church of Pocantico Hills was really something. Even tourists stopped to see the stained-glass windows created by two modern artists, Matisse and Chagall. Not that Tony knew squat about either of them, but he'd read the literature put out for tourists. Today the place was off-limits on account of the wedding. The Sheas obviously had some major clout in Tarrytown.

Impressive circle of friends, too, who stood off to the side in their expensive suits and silk dresses and pearls. Tony recognized several faces from the legal community. Couldn't place their names. He'd seen them on the news or in the newspaper.

"Excuse me, sir. Stand here, please." The tall, thin hawkish-looking photographer gestured for Tony to stand beside Dakota.

The guy didn't have to ask him twice. Tony sidled up beside her, their arms and hips touching, and inhaled her mysterious scent. Maybe he'd sniffed a little too enthusiastically because she gave him an annoyed look. Or maybe it was the touching part she didn't like.

"Dallas looks beautiful," he whispered while the photographer got everyone else into place.

Dakota immediately softened. "And happy."

"Is it gonna seem weird that she's married?"

"Not really." She shrugged, her arm rubbing his. "Nothing will change."

Tempted to ask about tonight's plan, he kept his mouth shut while the photographer finished positioning everyone. Tom stood too close to risk him hearing of the counterattack.

"Everyone ready?" The photographer clicked off two shots.

For the next twenty minutes, they were separated, pushed back together, coupled, shuffled from one stained-glass window to the next, the entire time the photographer muttering how difficult this was with everyone chatting and laughing.

Mrs. Shea stood back, commiserating, shaking her head and sliding her husband long-suffering looks. The honorable Judge Shea didn't seem to give a crap. Good for him.

Once the photographer was satisfied, or maybe because Dallas had whispered something to him, they disbanded and got into the waiting limos. The guests followed in their separate cars and everyone headed for the reception at the Shea's country club.

Tony was lucky enough to share a limo with Dakota. Too bad Nancy, Trudie and Wendy climbed in behind them. Could've been worse. He could've gotten stuck with Mr. and Mrs. Shea, and Cody and his snotty society date.

"Hey, how do you like being surrounded by all these women?" Wendy asked, while trying to get her long legs into a suitable position. She was a dancer, an extra on Broadway if he remembered correctly.

He stretched an arm out along the back of the seat and got comfortable, then gave her a cocky grin. "I can handle it."

"I bet you can." She gave him an inviting smile he wished Dakota had given him.

But she sat across from him with her face turned toward the window and didn't even react to what was going on.

Until Wendy said, "Hey, Dakota, I guess you're next."

"Next?"

"To bite the dust." Wendy grinned at Dakota's wide-eyed expression. "Tie the knot. Whatever they say these days."

"Why me? You're older."

"Ouch."

Dakota grinned. "Shouldn't you be the one getting antsy? Watching that biological clock."

"Ruthless, aren't you?"

Trudie laughed. "That's what makes her a good lawyer."

Dakota's grin tapered off.

No one seemed to notice but Tony. They all kept teasing each other back and forth while Dakota shrank back against the seat. Good to know she was touchy about the lawyer thing. Not that he was stupid enough to repeat the jokes he'd heard. Okay, so maybe he would've let a couple slip, but now he knew.

"So is like everybody gonna stay dressed like this, or can we change?" Wendy asked as they turned off the street and onto the lush country club grounds.

"I don't know, but I was hoping somebody would ask." Nancy looked to the others, and then focused on Dakota.

"I doubt Dallas cares one way or the other," she said, "but we'd better wait until after dinner so the photographer can get the rest of the pictures."

"Yeah, we don't want your mom freaking out."

Wendy tugged at her dress. "The same moron who invented high heels must have come up with this gem."

"Fair is fair." Tony couldn't resist. Not that he was particularly fond of ties. In fact, he hardly ever wore them—only when he absolutely had to.

Wendy smiled at him. "You are so damn cute. I can't believe Dallas kept you from us all these years."

Heat crawled up Tony's neck. Thankfully he knew he wouldn't turn red. He didn't embarrass easily but Wendy was something else.

"Now that Dallas has ditched me, I'm looking for a roommate if you're interested." Wendy gave him an impish grin, shifting so that their legs touched.

"Hey, he's already taken," Nancy said, rubbing a familiar shoulder against his.

He gave her a sharp look. So did Dakota.

Nancy laughed. "My six-year-old thinks he's it. She lights up like the Fourth of July every time she sees him."

Tony reared his head back. "Megan's six already?"

"Yep, she had a birthday two months ago."

"Man, then I haven't seen her in almost a year."

"You should come by sometime." Nancy smiled. "It would make her day."

"Yeah, maybe next weekend. I owe her a teddy bear for her birthday."

Wendy spoke up. "Nanc, I didn't know you were married. I thought you were one of us." When she frowned, Wendy added, "You know, single."

"I'm divorced," Nancy replied. "Does that count?"

"Oh, yeah. Definitely." Wendy peered out the

window at the impeccably manicured greens and small man-made lakes, stretching on for acres. "Wow, this place is awesome." She looked at Dakota. "Do you know if any Broadway people were invited?"

Dakota shrugged. "I don't think so."

"Just the boring legal types, huh?"

Trudie groaned and darted a look at Dakota. "Wendy, would you shut up?"

Dakota just laughed. "I know what you mean." She faked a yawn. "Bunch of long-winded, pontificating blowhards."

Everyone got quiet and stared at her.

Tilting her head to the side and smiling, Dakota added, "With a few exceptions, of course."

God, she was gorgeous. Tony just stared. He couldn't look away. With that soft smile on her peach-tinted lips, the way the late-afternoon sun filtered into the windows and lit her hair, she should have been spread out across a billboard. Wouldn't matter what product she peddled. Hell, even nail clippers. Any red-blooded guy would buy it.

Obviously he wasn't the only one with that opinion because Wendy said, "Jeez, Dakota, why aren't you modeling like Dallas?"

"I like what I do."

"You can practice law later. Make the easy bucks now while you still have the looks."

Trudie shook her head with disgust. Apparently she also noticed Dakota's defensive posture. "What part of keep quiet don't you understand?"

"Come on, Trudie, I'm just saying—"

"Hey, we're here. There's Dallas and Eric." Tony's timely interruption was met by a quick smile from Dakota. He winked back and she abruptly turned away, and he could've sworn her cheeks had started to pinken.

But she hid it while stepping out of the limo and leading them to the foyer to stand in the reception line where people were already waiting to congratulate the bride and groom.

Why the rest of the wedding party had to stand there was beyond him. Nobody cared if they were there or not. But now wasn't the time to question the tradition so he obediently positioned himself between Nancy and Trudie as Mrs. Shea instructed.

After more pictures were taken and everyone had had a crack at Dallas and Eric, the wedding party was finally allowed to enter the private dining room. More like a ballroom with tables and chairs for at least a hundred and fifty guests. Fresh flower arrangements, mostly orchids, were everywhere. Two bars were set up on either side of the room, manned by bartenders wearing tuxedos. He couldn't imagine how much this had set the Sheas back. Of course that kind of money was no sweat to them.

"Hey, where are the balloons?" he asked Dakota.

She gave him a weird look as if she hoped he was kidding but wasn't sure. And then surprised him by asking, "Do you want a drink?"

"Sure."

"Come on."

He followed as she led him around the guests who had already lined up in front of the bars. Several white-gloved waiters stood to the side and she whispered something to the short husky one who nodded and smiled ecstatically as if she'd just agreed to have his children.

Tony watched the guy abruptly turn around and then disappear through a side door that blended with the wall and had been invisible to Tony. "Where's he going?"

"To get our drinks."

"Ah." He nodded. "Come here often, do you?"

She arched a brow at him. "You want to wait in that line?"

"No, ma'am."

"All right then."

"Do we stay right here and wait or is there a rendezvous point?"

A smile tugged at her lips. "Don't worry. You won't get mobbed. This is a very civil bunch. They'll only complain to management."

"That I can handle. By the way, tell me you didn't order me champagne."

"I didn't order you champagne."

"Not to sound ungrateful."

"Uh-huh."

The waiter reappeared holding a small tray in one hand, and used the other to hand Dakota a glass of white wine and Tony a bottle of beer, his usual. Without a glass, too. Obviously she'd noticed what he was drinking last night.

The weekend was starting to look up.

Maybe she planned on taking Dallas up on her offer of a free minivacation with him. Before bringing it up, he glanced over his shoulder to make sure Tom wasn't around. No, but Wendy was headed their way.

Damn.

The only consolation was that Dakota looked just as disappointed.

Her red hair windblown, Wendy smelled faintly of tobacco as she approached. She looked from the glasses in their hands to the increasingly long line at the bar. "Where did you get the drinks?"

Dakota gestured vaguely over her shoulder. "A waiter was walking around with a tray."

"Cool." Wendy wandered off in the direction Dakota had sent her.

Tony chuckled.

"I didn't lie."

He didn't care. She'd gotten rid of Wendy. That's what counted. Not that he didn't like Wendy, but he wanted Dakota to himself. He wanted to lose himself in those sexy gray-blue eyes, and bask in the anticipation of tonight. Miles away from here. Alone. Nothing to do but get to know one another. Spend long leisurely hours of exploring each other's bodies.

That line of thinking had to stop. He shifted his weight from one foot to the other, trying to stop the blood from rushing south. He took a healthy gulp of icy cold beer and then met Dakota's amused eyes.

Dakota smiled and took another sip, her lashes long and thick resting on her cheeks. She barely wore any makeup, didn't have to. Her features were almost perfect. High cheekbones, a pert nose, full lips, her skin so flawless it was almost translucent. Her eyes were smaller than Dallas's, more gray than blue and deeper set, but she was every bit as gorgeous.

Man, he'd like to see the faces of everyone the first time she walked into a courtroom. Not the typical lawyer, that's for sure. Unless she always dressed for work the way she had last night, conservative and drab.

A trio of violinists in the corner started playing elevator music, but at least they kept it low-key. Up front there were two stages, one slightly elevated with band equipment and the other a parquet dance floor.

"Uh-oh." Tony saw Mrs. Shea heading toward them with obvious purpose. "I think we're about to be summoned."

Dakota looked over her shoulder, immediately tensing. "I have a feeling she wants me."

Interesting how tense she got at the mention of her mother. He knew a little bit from Dallas about the formidable Mrs. Shea, prominent college professor and demanding mother. The woman had done one really good thing for her girls. She'd encouraged them to go for an education instead of trade on their extraordinary looks. Had to give her credit for that.

Dakota sighed. "I'd better go see what she wants."

"I have a better idea. Let's take a walk."

She looked at him, the disbelief in her eyes slowly fading to uncertainty. "We just got here."

"So. Do you want to ditch her or not?"

Her lips parted in indignation, but a flicker of excitement sparked in her eyes. She briefly glanced over her shoulder again, caught her mother gaining on them and said, "Let's go."

3

DAKOTA LED Tony out of the banquet room to a side patio, knowing she'd pay hell for the disappearing act. In fact, she wouldn't put it past her mother to hunt them down. Except it was getting cold outside, with nothing on the fairway to block the biting wind, enough that it might insure them some privacy.

She swallowed. Was that what she wanted? To be out here alone with him? This was foolish. She knew how it would turn out. They wouldn't just talk. Facing him, she smiled. "Bad idea. It's a little too cool."

"Here." He shrugged out of his jacket, the white dress shirt straining against his broad chest. "Put this on."

"No, really, that's okay. Then you'll be cold. Let's go back—"

He slipped the jacket over her shoulders, and then turned her to face him. Unfortunately, she couldn't see his expression. The patio was very dimly lit by a pale blue glow, courtesy of the parade of solar lights staked along the perimeter. The thought infused her with a dangerous excitement that made her nipples tighten and her resolve weaken.

"This should keep you warm." He pulled the lapels together and she stumbled toward him, steadying herself with her palms against his chest.

"Sorry," she whispered and straightened, reluctantly letting her hands fall away.

He released the lapels and cupped her shoulders, then ran his palms down her arms. "You smell good."

She shivered when his warm breath fanned her cheek, and he took her cold hands, sandwiching them between his slightly callused ones. She'd never been with a man with work-roughened hands. How would they feel touching the tenderest part of her body? Stroking the area around her nipples? The soft skin between her thighs?

He lowered his head and her breath caught when his lips brushed hers. But only briefly before he whispered, "I can't wait for later."

"Later?"

The sound of the French doors opening had them guiltily jumping apart. Thankfully it was Dallas, the long white gown obvious even in the dim light.

"Hey, you guys, dinner is going to be served in twenty minutes."

Dakota sighed. "You came out here to tell us that?"

"Better me than Mother. Anyway, Dakota, I need to talk to you."

"Now?"

"Yep. Sorry, Tony. I need her for five minutes."

He gestured with his hand. "I'll see you inside."

"Here's your jacket," Dakota said, pushing it off her shoulders and then handing it to him.

"Keep it while you're outside."

"I'm not staying out here. It's cold."

"Trust me," Dallas said, "it would be better if we talked out here."

Dakota didn't like the sound of that. Even Tony frowned as he tried to give her back his jacket. She shook her head. "I'm okay."

After shooting Dallas a curious look, he left them alone. Dakota was pretty curious herself. "What's going on?"

"I have a favor to ask of you."

"Okay."

"It's kind of big, but I really, really need you to do this for me," Dallas said. "Okay?"

"Well, what is it?"

"Promise me you'll do it first."

Dakota snorted. "Right."

"Come on, Dakota, have I ever asked you for anything? You're my sister. It's my wedding, and I need this favor badly."

"What already?" She waited, but Dallas's chin stubbornly went up, and the truth was Dakota would never refuse her sister anything. "All right. I promise."

"I need you to play decoy for me tonight after the reception."

"Why?"

"You know how Eric's friend Tom likes to play practical jokes. We're pretty sure he's going to try and sabotage our honeymoon."

Dakota shook her head at her sister's paranoia. "He wouldn't do something so juvenile."

"He'd think it was hilarious. I know him, and you need to help me out." Dallas rubbed her bare arms. "It is cold out here."

"So you want me to do what exactly?" Dakota asked as her sister linked an arm through hers and steered her toward the entry into the banquet room.

Dallas opened the door and the light inside illuminated her smile. "Go on my honeymoon for me. With Tony."

DAMN THAT Dallas. As soon as they got inside someone called to her sister and she was off with no further explanation other than she'd already packed a bag for Dakota. As if the matter were settled.

Dakota headed straight for the bathroom, her thoughts spinning so quickly she literally felt dizzy. Or maybe it was the excitement of what lay ahead? The whole idea was crazy. And perfect. A weekend with Tony? She couldn't have come up with a better plan herself. Except she had a lot going on at work, and it wasn't as if she could just *not* show up on Monday.

Two older women, colleagues of her mother whom she vaguely knew, stood at the mirror talking and applying lipstick. Dakota smiled at them and then hurried into a stall, put the seat down and sat on the john. She hadn't even asked her sister if Tony knew about the plan and if he'd agreed to go. Is that what he'd meant by "later"? She straightened. If he'd known about this before she had that would really tick her off.

She took a deep breath. Dallas had purposely

waited to tell her. Just so she wouldn't have time to come up with an excuse not to go. She was a coward. She admitted it.

Dallas was the independent one. She did as she pleased. Dakota, however, was the good little lamb. Always doing what she was told.

She still didn't like it that Dallas had conspired with Tony. For that reason alone she ought to tell her sister to find some other flunky. Yeah, right. Like she wasn't ready to leave the reception right now, get him alone and rip off his clothes.

Feeling a little flushed, she bent over, crossing her arms over her knees and breathing deeply. She was crazy for even considering doing this. But she'd be even crazier for refusing the opportunity. The ladies' room door opened and she heard someone murmur about dinner starting. She had to go or someone would surely come looking for her.

Straightening, she smoothed back her hair, and then checked the front of her dress. Smiling, she stood, ready for the games to begin. She'd go but that didn't mean she'd go easily.

"Guess what Mother wants." Dallas met her partway.

Tony followed Dallas, who gave him an exasperated look.

Dakota sensed an undercurrent but they didn't seem angry with each other. "What?"

"To change the seating."

"I would've guessed that."

Dallas snorted. "I'm having the big formal wedding like she wanted, and I kept my mouth shut when she invited half the legal and academic communities, most of whom I don't know. But that's it."

"Calm down." Tony slipped an arm around her shoulders and squeezed lightly. "That's one of the first rules of weddings. Mothers get to show off their kids and put their husbands in the poorhouse. Just ask my pop."

Dallas rolled her eyes. "Gee, if I'd known that was a rule I wouldn't have gotten upset."

"Now you know."

Sighing, she smiled and kissed Tony on the cheek. "Entertain my sister, okay?"

"I don't need entertaining," Dakota said, but Dallas had already flitted over to another couple Dakota didn't recognize. She turned toward Tony. "I don't—"

"I know." His mouth curved in a sexy grin that made her heart skip a beat. "So entertain me instead."

"BETTER TAKE IT EASY with that stuff." Tony eyed the brandy snifter in Dakota's hand, her second cognac as far as he could tell. And that was after several glasses of wine with dinner. A different variety was served with each course. Him, he stuck to his beer. Two glasses of wine and he'd be kissing the floor. For some reason, the stuff really got to him.

"One mother is all I can handle, thank you very much." She took a deliberate sip, smiled and said, "I'm fine. Really."

"Okay," he said without conviction. The fact that

she'd said that a little too loudly was proof enough she better give the booze a rest.

Although he had to admit she wasn't sloppy. If he hadn't been sitting next to her at dinner he wouldn't have known she'd had that much wine. Plus each course had been spaced out so that dinner had ended up being the longest, most quiet meal in history. At least for his family. When the San Angelos got together for a party, talking, eating and dancing were not mutually exclusive.

They'd finally finished dessert a half hour ago, and people had started dancing the moment the band struck the first note. He wanted to ask Dakota to dance but the song had to be just the right one. Despite his mouthing off, he wasn't all that swift on the dance floor. The beat had to be slow and easy so he didn't have to think too much about what his feet were doing.

He'd skip the idea altogether, but the way Mrs. Shea had been giving him the eye, he figured dancing with Dakota would be the only way he'd get close to her. Dallas and Eric were already out there and so were Trudie and Wendy who'd pulled Tom along with them. At the end of the table, Serena and Nancy seemed deep in conversation.

The song ended and the band eased into another, slower, moodier one he could handle. He turned to Dakota but her father beat him to it.

Mr. Shea was taking her by the hand. "Hope you saved a dance for your old man," he said, smiling fondly at his daughter.

"*Save* a dance? No one's asked me yet," she said, with a teasing smile at Tony as she set down her brandy.

"My mistake." He met her eyes. "I claim the next one."

Laughing, she got to her feet and allowed her father to lead her to the dance floor. The way that dress hugged her curves bordered on illegal. Her hips moved with a little extra enthusiasm almost as if for his benefit. Hard not to stare, but he sensed someone over his shoulder and looked up.

"Mind if I sit with you for a moment?" Mrs. Shea didn't wait for an answer. She lowered herself gracefully into Dakota's chair.

"Gee, here I thought you were going to ask me to dance."

She smiled and gazed out toward the dance floor. "Everyone seems to be having a good time."

"Yes, ma'am. Free liquor does it every time."

Annoyance flickered in her eyes. One blink and it was gone.

He tried not to smile and sipped his beer.

"Didn't you like the wine we selected?"

"I'm sure it was just fine. I prefer beer."

"Ah." She turned again to watch the dancers.

The woman hardly looked as if she could have three adult children. Tall, blond and trim, she didn't look much over forty. In fact, she could've passed for Dallas and Dakota's sister.

She caught him staring.

Tony coughed. "I was just thinking how you look more like your daughters' sister. They'll be lucky to look like you in twenty years," he said and meant it. She was a very attractive woman.

She looked annoyed again, her pinched expression adding a decade to her face. "Looks hardly make the person."

"Couldn't agree more." Tony took another sip of beer to avoid saying something sarcastic. Like her being a perfect example.

"Take Dakota." Mrs. Shea's gaze went to her daughter. "She could have had a successful modeling career. But she was smart enough to realize the foolhardiness of such a move. Wisely she chose to further her education, secure her future." She looked at him then, steadily meeting his gaze. "Did you know she's got a good shot at a judgeship?"

"Yeah, I heard something about it from Dallas. The thing I don't understand is that she's only been out of law school for what—three, four years? I'm sure she's really bright and I don't know how the system works but isn't that kind of fast?" He smiled and brought his beer to his lips. "But then again your husband probably has connections if that's what you two want for Dakota," he said before taking a long pull.

He had to give the woman credit for keeping a straight face. Maybe she should've been the attorney. The only sign that he'd dented her composure was that it took her a few moments to come back with, "Where did you attend college, Mr. San Angelo?"

"NYU. And call me Tony." He enjoyed the surprise on her face. Probably figured he hadn't made it through high school. Yet she wouldn't be disappointed for long.

"What was your degree in?"

Ah, well, the fun lasted all of thirty seconds. "I dropped out the middle of my sophomore year."

Her eyebrows went up. "Really?" He didn't think he imagined an inkling of satisfaction on her face. "May I ask why?"

He shook his head. "School just wasn't for me. I like working with my hands."

"Yes, but—"

He held up a hand. "No offense, Professor Shea, I understand where you're coming from but that's the way it is. I like what I do. I'm not going to change my mind."

"Forgive me. I didn't mean to sound as if I'm interfering. We all make our own choices."

The song ended and Dakota and her father headed back toward them. Even from this distance he could see the alarm on Dakota's face, and surprisingly what looked like disapproval in her father's.

Mrs. Shea pushed back her chair. "I suppose we were lucky all of our children valued their education." She smiled at him as she rose to her feet. "Nice chatting with you, Tony."

Tempted to remind her of Dallas's detour he decided to keep his mouth shut. It didn't matter. He got the message. He lived on the wrong side of the fence.

She slipped away a second before Dakota returned to her seat. Her father nodded at Tony and then followed his wife back to their table.

Frowning, Dakota watched until they both sat down. "What was that about?"

"What?"

She fixed him with a pretty intimidating glare. One she'd probably perfected in court. "What did my mother want?"

He grinned and got up, pulling her with him. "She wanted me to dance with you."

"Right."

He was lucky. The song was slow. He shouldn't have too much trouble keeping up. They got to the center of the floor and he guided them to the middle for some privacy. Not much, but better than having her mother's gaze boring into his back as he slid both his arms around Dakota, his hands resting just above the curve of her sweet little backside. No holding one hand out in the air crap. He wanted to feel her chest pressed against him. Feel her thighs move with his.

She sighed softly, and then tilted her head back to look at him. "Come on. What did she want?"

No way was he getting into this conversation with her. He couldn't without bad-mouthing her mother, and he wasn't doing that. "Why isn't your brother being groomed to be a judge?"

Her lips parted slightly as she hesitated, and if they were anywhere else, he would've accepted the invitation. And if she didn't quit soon…

"Cody is far too mercenary, hardly civil servant material." She laughed softly and swept a quick glance around. "Oops, did I say that?"

Civil servant? That stopped Tony. He hadn't thought of it that way. "Defense attorneys make more money, huh?"

"Oh, please." She chuckled and then squinted at him. "Are you kidding?"

He shrugged. "How would I know?"

"Defense attorneys can make oodles of money. Especially defending white-collar clients." She whispered. "My brother's favorite kind of criminal."

"What happened to innocent until proven guilty?"

"I wasn't referring to the innocent ones." She paused thoughtfully. "Although they usually end up racking up a lot more legal fees."

"You're so cute when you're being materialistic."

"Hey." She lightly pinched his shoulder. "I was being analytical."

"Oh." He smiled and brought her closer so that she pressed her cheek against the base of his throat. His lips were touching her forehead. This is where he wanted her. Not leaning away from him analyzing the legal profession.

Besides, the dance floor had gotten more crowded. Good for him. It gave him an excuse to draw her closer. Bad for her in that she could be overheard and, since half the people there were either lawyers, judges or somehow related, she'd be better off zipping it.

Her arms tightened around his neck and she rubbed her cheek against his jaw. His body immediately reacted. If the song suddenly ended and he had to walk back to the table, he'd be screwed.

"Hello, Dakota."

She lifted her head and smiled at the distinguished-looking older man dancing beside them with a much younger blond woman. "Hi, Judge Hawkins."

He nodded to Tony and then said to Dakota, "We're not in the courtroom. I think it would be okay to call me David."

"That would feel a little too strange."

He smiled, nodded and they moved apart, but not before the man gave Tony a sizing up.

Tony ignored him. "Is that his wife?"

"Nope. He's divorced. Three times now."

"He looks old enough to be her father."

"Probably is. He likes them young."

He obviously liked Dakota, but Tony didn't point that out. The song wound down and he hoped like hell the band would stick to a slow beat. They did and everyone on the dance floor stayed. Several other couples crowded in and damned if they didn't all seem to know Dakota. Their once-private area was getting to be as bad as Grand Central Station.

When it was announced that it was time to cut the cake, he didn't even mind. Maybe after that they could get out of here. Even if he and Dakota just rode to the airport together, alone, no parents, no coworkers, and the evening ended there, he'd be okay with that. Not happy, but okay.

Glasses of champagne were passed out while Dallas and Eric got ready to cut the cake. Dallas got a little impatient when the photographer kept trying to reposition them and she dug into the cake with her fingers and offered the piece to Eric. Everyone laughed. Except Mrs. Shea, but that was no surprise.

In Tony's experience, shortly after the cake was cut the bride and groom usually left the reception.

That meant he and Dakota would be leaving, too. He glanced at his watch. No matter, they'd have to leave within half an hour to get to LaGuardia in time for their flight.

An older, distinguished-looking man had intercepted Dakota right before the cake cutting, and Tony scanned the room locating her in time to see her drain a flute of champagne and exchange it for another. She caught his eye and smiled, then raised the glass to him before gulping down half the contents.

What the hell? Was she on some kind of mission to get plastered? Maybe she didn't like flying? A lot of people didn't. Better that be the reason than anything personal. He wanted to be with her this weekend, but not if she had to get loaded to be with him.

"We're going to have to leave soon." Dallas dabbed at the white frosting clinging to the corner of her mouth. "Where's Dakota?"

"Over there."

"Ah, she's talking to Judge Mayfield and his wife. She shouldn't be long. We'll meet at the door in fifteen minutes. Eric is having the limo brought around front."

"Is she okay?" he asked.

Dallas smiled "Yes. Trust me."

That's about all he could do. "I'll be ready." His gaze went to Dakota.

She was laughing at something the judge said, her face slightly flushed. She tossed her hair back over her shoulder, the honey-colored strands catching the light from the chandelier. The red dress shimmered as she moved, emphasizing the tempting curve of her backside. Yeah, he was ready all right. He had been from the first time he saw her.

"WHO EVER HEARD of a limo without champagne?" Dakota sighed, hiked her dress up to her thighs and then swung her legs up on the seat where she sat opposite Tony. Predictably his gaze went straight to the hem of her dress, and then ran down the length of her legs. "We'll simply have to have the driver stop for some." She lifted her fist to knock on the dividing glass, but Tony lunged from his seat and captured her wrist.

"Don't you think you've had enough to drink?" He got up and joined her on her seat, using his hip to nudge her legs aside.

"Excuse me?" She indignantly lifted her chin, and slightly slurred her words then asked, "Do you think I'm drunk?"

He hesitated, exhaling in exasperation, and she had to really struggle to keep a straight face. "Look, we can't stop. We'll miss our plane."

"Plane? What plane?"

He stared at her. "You're kidding, right?"

"Of course I'm kidding." She pulled her hem up a little higher and used her pointed toes to trace a path across his back. "Remind me."

"Oh, God," he muttered, passing a hand over his face, and then covering his mouth and exhaling loudly.

"What's the matter?"

"Nothing."

"Why are you still holding my wrist?"

"What? Oh, sorry."

As soon as he let go, she knocked on the dividing glass.

"Yes, ma'am?" The driver's voice immediately came over the intercom.

Tony pressed the response button. "Sorry, my mistake. We're fine."

"Hey, I wanted—"

Tony cut her off with a brief kiss, and then whispered, "When we get on the plane you can have all the champagne you want."

She slipped her arms around his neck and pulled him closer. "What if I want something else?"

His breath warm and uneven against her cheek, he said, "Such as?"

She shifted so that her hip rubbed him right where it counted, and he tensed. She made him wait a few seconds and then whispered, "Chocolate."

"Ah…" He chuckled softly. "When we get to the airport you can have that, too."

"For now I'll settle for a kiss."

"You will, huh?"

She nodded, and then waited, surprised by the uncertainty in his eyes. Maybe it was a trick of the shadows, or maybe he didn't want to take advantage of her because he thought she was drunk. The idea softened her and she tightened her arms around his neck, bringing him close enough that their noses touched. She slanted her head and met his lips.

His reluctance lasted all of a second before he kissed her back, going down with her when she laid back against the cushioned seat. The tinted dividing window prevented the driver from seeing anything and it would be easy to get carried away. Especially with Tony's broad chest pressed to her breasts, his arousal growing against her lower belly. But they were too close to the airport and if she really wanted to torment him, now was the time.

He'd conspired with Dallas and deserved a helping of torture. Just a little before they got down to the good stuff, she reminded herself, when he parted her lips with his tongue and her determination started to evaporate. She moved her left thigh to rub his hard-on and he groaned against her mouth.

She hadn't planned on torturing herself, too, but every pore in her body had come alive, her nipples so ripe they ached, and it was a good thing she'd opened her eyes in time to see the first sign for LaGuardia. Knowing they were about to be interrupted, she reached for his zipper. And then secretly smiled when he groaned, and stilled her hand.

"THE CAPTAIN HAS turned off the seat belt sign and you're free to move around the cabin. However, if you remain in your seat, we ask that you keep your seat belt fastened. Thank you."

The flight attendant had barely finished her spiel and Dakota reached for her seat belt.

Tony stopped her. "Where are you going?"

She gave him a sleepy smile and twisted around in her seat to face him. "Nowhere."

Neither of them had a coat so he'd given her his

jacket to wear over the dress but this particular position gave him a sneak preview that he didn't need right now. She'd gotten him so damn worked up in the limo that he didn't trust his cock anymore.

Getting checked in had cooled him off. Replaying the scene in his head helped do it again. The ticket agent looked as if she thought he was kidnapping Dakota. Fortunately she pulled it together long enough to provide her identification and tell everyone who'd listen that they were on their honeymoon.

"Where are we going?" she asked, and promptly covered a yawn.

"Dakota. You know where we're going. Dallas talked to you, remember?"

She blinked at him. "Sort of."

God, he didn't like this. He cleared his throat. "What exactly do you remember?"

"She packed a bag for me, right?"

He nodded.

"Did she remember my toothbrush?" She yawned again. "My electric one."

"I'm sure she did."

"I think I'll take a nap now."

"Good idea."

She shifted so that she could lay her head on his shoulder, and with one hand he shook out a blanket the flight attendant had given them earlier. He draped it over her, and she snuggled closer.

Man, he sure hoped Dallas knew what she was doing. She swore Dakota wasn't drunk. Just a little tipsy. That she understood exactly where she was

going. And who she was with. Because if she didn't,
this weekend or any chance they might have had was
going to be so messed up.

4

"THANKS, OTIS. I'll take it from here."

"May I get you some ice, sir?"

Tony shook his head. "Nah, we're okay." He tipped the bellman three times what he normally would, hoping the guy didn't call security. Or worse, the police. All the way up on the elevator ride, he'd eyed Tony as if he were Jack the Ripper. Not that he blamed the older man. The way Dakota was acting, everyone from the flight attendant to the cab driver had to be wondering if Tony had drugged her.

He'd practically had to hold her up just to get her off the plane. And then she was so disoriented she kept asking where she was up until three minutes ago when they'd arrived at the suite.

"Do I have any clothes?" Dakota asked, yawned and then stretched, before sinking onto the couch.

Otis stopped on his way to the door and slowly turned around. "May I assist you in any way, miss?" he asked solemnly, his gaze steadily on her and deliberately away from Tony.

She'd taken off his jacket in the taxi and the way she sat, her dress slightly askew, exposed a lot of cleavage. Her lips curved in a teasing smile. "I don't think so. We're on our honeymoon."

The relief on the man's face was almost laughable. "Ah, I see. Very good." Backing toward the door, he looked approvingly at Tony. "Very good, sir. I'll bid you good-night then."

"See ya, Otis." Tony hurried to double lock the door as soon as the man was gone. When he turned back to Dakota, she had her eyes closed.

She looked pale against the navy-blue-and-cream floral cushions. But a couple of days on a sunny beach would fix that. The problem now was whether he should leave her here in the living room.

"Dakota," he said low enough not to wake her if she was sleeping.

She sighed and snuggled down deeper into the cushions, letting one of her high heels slide off her foot. Her feet were long, narrow but dainty, and shining through the sheer black hose her toenails were a bright red.

Her tousled hair looked more sexy than messy, and thinking of how soft and warm and willing she'd been in the limo had him itching to get down to business. But not when she was like this. Coffee. Strong and black. He wondered if that really worked.

He looked away and studied the living room. The tropic-styled suite had to have cost a small fortune. Tony was no expert on decorating or art but he knew about wood and carpentry and the hardwood floors alone had set the owner back a year's rent for a Queens apartment. Anyone could tell that the rattan furniture was of the highest quality and the artwork on the walls and interesting native pieces casually set on corner pedestals weren't cheap knockoffs. Expensive knockoffs maybe.

Even the bar area was no afterthought. At least ten feet across against a mirrored wall, the back shelf was stocked with full-size bottles of premium brands and not the miniature version. The refrigerator was full size, too, and loaded with different varieties of beer, according to Otis. Four bar stools with blue-and-cream-colored seats that matched the couch were arranged around the tall, curved rattan bar.

No fake plants either. Eight-foot palms stood on either side of the sliding glass door to the balcony. It was dark but he knew they faced the ocean. Not just because the front desk clerk had told him. Tony could hear the waves lapping the shore.

Man, it sucked that Dallas and Eric had spent all this money and Tom was screwing up their plans. No doubt they had something equally nice someplace else but that wasn't the point. It wasn't even about the money. Tony had already decided he'd pay for the suite and everything else this weekend. He didn't care what Dallas said. But it was all the hassle she'd gone through to counter Tom's prank that irritated Tony.

He couldn't think about that right now. It pissed him off too much and he had another problem to consider…sobering up Dakota. His gaze went back to Dakota. For a second he thought he saw her eyes open, but as he moved closer he realized it had to have been a trick of the light.

He'd already lost the bow tie and shrugged out of the jacket. He draped it over the rattan chair that matched the couch and bar stools, and then grabbed their bags and carried them to the bedroom.

The friggin' bedroom was almost as big as the living room, with a canopied king-size bed and one of those white nettings you only see in movies draped over it and tied back to the bedposts. There was another couch and another sliding glass door that led to a separate balcony. More palms, more paintings.

He found the large walk-in closet and placed their bags on the built-in luggage racks. Kicking off his shoes, he unfastened his belt at the same time and then hung it on a gold-plated hook behind the door. He pulled his shirt from the waistband of his pants and started unbuttoning it as he walked out into the bedroom.

Dakota stood in the doorway, leaning against the frame. Frowning slightly, she tried to smooth her hair. A few curls sprang back to rest on her cheek. "Tony?"

"Yeah?"

"Where are we?"

He cleared his throat. "You don't remember anything."

"Well, yes, of course I do." Her gaze slid down to his exposed chest, lingered for a long satisfying moment.

"What exactly do you remember?"

"The wedding."

"I hope so." He chuckled. "And?"

She put two fingers to her temple. "Wow, do I have a headache."

"Yeah, a vat of wine will do that."

She gave him a glare that was immensely reassuring. Yup, she was definitely coming around.

He grinned. "Let's see if Dallas packed any aspirin for you."

He brought the bag from closet and set it on the bed, then left her to root through it while he went to get some water from the bar.

The refrigerator was stocked with Evian and Perrier. He grabbed two Evians, one for each of them, and then returned to the room.

She shook her head. "No aspirin."

"Wait a minute. Let me check in here." The place had everything else and he wouldn't be surprised if the bathroom was stocked with personal items.

He slowed as he entered and let out a low whistle. He'd seen some fancy bathrooms before but this was totally awesome. A huge bathtub with three marble steps leading up to it. The entire floor was cream-and-tan marble. Not the cheesy fake kind either. The tub and dual vanity fixtures were gold and in the corner was a glass shower large enough for three people.

If you were into that kind of thing. Tony was a simple man. He just wanted Dakota. Naked. In that tub. Or shower. It didn't matter. As long as it was with him.

"Tony?"

The sound of her voice made him jerk. "What?"

"What's taking you so—oh, my." She walked past

him, her fascinated gaze sweeping the room. "I definitely could get used to this."

"You mean you don't have one at home?"

"I wish." She swayed a little but other than that she seemed steady and coherent.

"I haven't checked to see if there's any aspirin."

"A shower," she said. "That's what I need."

"Good idea." He backed toward the door. "I'll call room service. Order some coffee."

"Wait. I need help with this zipper." She gave him her back.

He moved in and found the small tab and slowly drew it down, his heart thumping at each inch of pale silky skin he exposed. She wasn't wearing a bra, which surprised him; she was so firm and high he'd had no idea. As he pulled the zipper down past the curve of her backside, he saw that she was wearing a red thong.

Drawing in a sharp breath, he stepped back. "Anything else?"

She slid her arms from the sleeves, and then holding the dress over her breasts, she turned around. "Thank you."

"You're welcome." He looked into her eyes, found them focused and aware, and leaned toward her.

She met his lips, tentatively at first, brushing lightly, using the tip of her tongue gently along his lower lip. His groin tightened. But then she slipped her tongue into his mouth and pursued him with an eagerness that brought him to his senses.

This wasn't Dakota. This was the booze talking.

The last thing he wanted or needed was her mortification tomorrow morning.

With every shred of willpower he possessed, he pulled away.

"What's wrong?" She clutched the dress tighter.

"Want me to start the water for you?"

She lifted a shoulder, the move casual and sexy as hell. "Sure."

He rolled back his sleeve and stuck his hand in the shower to turn it on. The heat of her stare seared his back and he took his time getting the right water temperature while he tried to figure out just how noble he wanted to be.

"There you go." He dried his arm on a white fluffy towel and pulled his sleeve back down, carefully avoiding looking at her.

"I'm not drunk," she said, "if that's what you're worried about."

He looked at her, his cock twitching at the exposed curve of her bare hip the limp dress didn't cover. "You had a lot to drink."

"Not as much as you think."

He smiled, but then she moistened her lips, the tip of her pink tongue leaving a tempting sheen across her lower lip and he totally lost track of rational thought.

"Want to join me?" she whispered.

He cleared his throat and ran a hand through his hair, and then caught sight of the reflection of her naked backside in the mirror. She had on the thong but that meant nothing. His cock sure as hell couldn't tell.

"Tony."

He looked into her confused eyes. He should say something, but nothing came to mind.

She sighed, and then covered a yawn. "If you're not going to join me, would you get out?"

He smiled, and then forced himself toward the door. The yawn and droopy eyelids had done it. Three more hours and the sun would be coming up. It wouldn't hurt either of them to grab a couple of hours of sleep. He'd take the couch for now. Tomorrow, when she'd be totally clearheaded, was another story.

WHAT THE HELL was Dallas thinking? Dakota started emptying the small bag her sister had packed for her. Two bikinis, one yellow, one red, both so itty-bitty she wasn't even sure how you put them on. The yellow gauzy strip was probably supposed to be a cover-up, although it sure wasn't going to cover up a damn thing.

Even the two pairs of khaki shorts were totally unacceptable. So brief you practically needed a Brazilian wax to wear them. And the halter tops and skimpy sundresses? Dakota shook her head. She'd have to find a hotel boutique first thing. She checked her watch. Nine-ten.

Her gaze was drawn to the bedroom door, the only thing separating her from Tony, and she automatically pulled the lapels of the robe together.

As much water as she'd had to drink last night, she'd apparently had more wine and champagne than she thought. Her head ached and remembering how brazen she'd been made her wince a little. Not that she'd changed her mind about having hot monkey sex with Tony. But she normally wasn't that out there about it. Probably served her right for carrying the tipsy thing so far.

Turned out the joke was on her. She could've been sleeping with Tony instead of alone. He got points for being honorable, but damn... Ironically, the knock came at that moment.

She drew in a deep breath. "Come in."

He opened the door. No shirt. No socks. Just last night's tuxedo pants. A beard-darkened jaw and a gorgeous expanse of muscled chest and pecs so well defined she wanted to run her hands over them. Touch his nubby brown nipples, the crisp swirling hair...

"I heard you so I knew you were up." He gestured toward the closet. "I need my bag."

"Of course."

"And the bathroom. The one out there doesn't have a shower."

She struggled to keep her eyes level with his. Not that he noticed. His gaze had lowered to her chest, and she realized she was clutching the robe so tightly her fingers were starting to ache.

She cleared her throat and released her death grip. "It's all yours. I've had my shower," she said, unnecessarily, considering her damp hair.

"I won't be long." On his way to the closet he stopped, and eyed the pile of clothes she'd left on the bed. "I hope Dallas included something for the beach."

"Um, not really."

"What's that?"

She followed his far-too-interested gaze to the yellow bikini. "My sister's idea of a joke."

He studied her for a moment. "I take it you remember everything now?"

"Of course I do." She started refolding the clothes, too embarrassed to meet his eyes. A shameful flashback to last night made her wish she were in court. She'd even be willing to face Judge Hadley, an attorney's worst nightmare. Anything but standing here, having to lie to Tony. On the other hand, she wasn't lying. She did remember. "I knew what was going on."

"Then you're okay with everything."

She didn't have to look at him to know he was grinning. She heard it in his voice. "I'm here, aren't I?"

"A little testy, aren't we? I heard that a Bloody Mary can take care of that hangover."

"I'm not hungover. I'm absolutely fine."

Hiding a smile, she replaced the clothes in the bag.

"What are you doing?"

Dakota looked at him, startled by his urgent tone. He still wasn't wearing a shirt. Not that she expected one to magically appear, but jeez, how was she supposed to talk to him? "Excuse me?"

"The suite is paid for—we have the rest of the weekend. Don't go."

"I—I'm not." She shrugged, flattered yet embarrassed at his desire for her to stay. "I was just putting away the clothes I won't be using."

A teasing grin curved his mouth. "I'm down with that. We'll stay naked the whole weekend."

"Funny." She tucked in the pseudo cover-up. "I'm going to the hotel boutique and pick up a few more suitable things to wear."

"What could Dallas have packed that's so bad?"

She half laughed, half groaned. "You have no idea. Wait till you see what's in your bag."

"I know what's in my bag." He ducked into the closet and carried out the black leather garment bag. "I packed it myself."

"Really?" She folded her arms across her chest. He'd have to admit the conspiracy now. "When?"

"Yesterday morning."

"Nice that you had that much notice."

He frowned at her. "I didn't know she was gonna ask you at the last minute. That had nothing to do with me."

Dakota sat on the edge of the bed, thinking it over. Now that she wasn't so annoyed or panicked it suddenly made sense. This was all her sister's doing. Dallas had given Tony warning because she figured he wouldn't turn her down. But she'd blindsided Dakota. Because Dallas knew she'd have found another way. Bless her! Dakota tried not to smile.

"Hey, don't get mad at Dallas." Tony set down the garment bag, and then sat next to her. "She had a lot on her mind. Probably thought she'd already asked you."

"You don't have to defend her." It was ridiculous how hard her heart pounded just because he'd sat next to her. Although he really hadn't left much space between them.

"She probably figured you needed a vacation. Working all those long hours like you do…"

"How do you know how much I work?"

"I know more than you think." He gave her one of those teasing winks that she was absurdly susceptible to, and then added, "Have you looked outside yet?"

She shook her head, and then hoped he didn't jump up to open the drapes.

He stayed right where he was, if anything, leaned a little closer. "Wait till you see it, Dakota, sky and water so clear and blue you'll want to pack up your Manhattan apartment and become a beach bum."

"I like the city. Besides, how do you know I live in Manhattan?"

"You look the type."

"Meaning?"

He smiled. "This isn't a courtroom. You can't interrupt. Okay, like I was saying, the sand is as white as fresh snow and the—"

"We live in the city. How would you know what fresh snow looks like?" She didn't know when he'd taken her hand. But he was doing this soothing stroking motion on the inside of her wrist.

"You keep interrupting and I'll have to do something about it."

"Oh, yeah?"

"Yeah." The stroking stopped.

He lowered his head and her heart pounded harder. All he did was brush his lips over hers and she thought her chest would explode. He slid his tongue inside and she hoped that whimper didn't come from her. When he put his hand on her thigh, turned out she didn't care.

She tentatively touched his chest, his skin taut and warm beneath her palm, the swirling hair just as soft and crisp as she'd imagined. His kiss deepened and the robe slid off her shoulder. She shivered, and his warm lips left hers to trail down the side of her neck, slowly making its way to her collarbone. His tongue swept the hollow and she shivered again. So violently that his head came up.

"Cold?"

She shook her head.

He smiled. "Sure? I can warm you up."

She smiled back. "You've already done that," she said and let the other side of the robe slip off her bare shoulder.

5

TONY'S MOUTH WENT DRY. God, she was beautiful. And soft. He'd never been with a woman with skin this amazingly soft. And he'd had his share. Especially in the early college days. But Dakota, she was something.

He used his forefinger to trace the exposed satiny skin at the edge of the robe. She didn't even flinch when his finger dipped lower, following the curve of her breast.

The front door buzzer sounded and he cursed himself. He'd forgotten he ordered room service. Did they have to be so efficient?

Dakota pulled away. "What was that?"

"I ordered coffee and rolls."

"Ah." She gathered the front of her robe together.

He hooked a finger under her chin, lifted it and lightly kissed her. "If we don't answer, they'll just leave it out there in the parlor."

The ringing turned to a persistent knock.

"Or not," he said wryly and pushed a hand through his hair. "I'll be right back," he said, getting to his feet, knowing the mood had taken a nosedive.

"I'll get dressed and come out for coffee."

He made a face. "Do you have to get dressed?"

She laughed, got up and gave him a small shove. "Out. I need caffeine."

"I'll show you what you need," he said, taking her hands and pulling her into his arms.

Her lips parted and a small sigh breached, drifting across his chin. She wove her arms around his neck and tilted her head back.

Another knock at the door.

Damn.

"I know," she said, and moved away. "I'll be out in a minute."

He wasn't happy about it but he went to the door and let in the obnoxiously cheerful waiter. Tony almost forgave him when he caught a whiff of a fresh croissant and the strong Colombian brew. After over-tipping the guy, Tony escorted the waiter to the door, cutting him off when he tried to advise Tony on the best fishing spots. Yeah, as if.

He took the tray to the table and poured them each a cup of coffee, thinking about Dakota and how different she was away from her family. He probably knew more than he should from Dallas. She wasn't a talker normally, but sometimes after the Sheas' monthly Saturday-night dinner, she'd just had to vent while they ate their lunches. Tony had never minded. It was kind of interesting hearing about a family so different from his own.

"I need caffeine, and I need it badly."

Tony looked up and nearly dropped his cup. Through the filmy thing she had tied around her, he could see strips of yellow. A bikini. A very, very tiny bikini. Over the knot where she'd tied the wrap, her breasts swelled. Not too much. Two perfect handfuls. Enough that all the blood rushed south and made his thoughts go crazy.

That was Dallas's doing. Man, he owed her. Big-time.

"This one mine?" Dakota picked up the other cup he'd poured.

"Uh, yeah."

She rooted through the condiments and plucked out a pink packet of sweetener and carefully sprinkled a dash of the white powder. "Cream?"

"Right here."

She splashed in some cream from the small silver pitcher and stirred, not once looking at him. "Do I smell banana bread?"

"I think there's some in that basket." He finally got it. She was actually self-conscious. Why, he didn't understand. She was perfect. "It's nice to see you in something other than a suit," he said calmly, and tried to focus on pouring himself more joe. "These puny cups are ridiculous. Two sips and that's it."

"Would you like me to order you a trough?" She flipped the red linen napkin over to get to the treats and peered inside the basket.

"That would be an improvement." While she was busy avoiding him, he took another heart-stopping look at her long legs. He had no idea what to say next. How to put her at ease, how to calm down his heated body. He deserved a friggin' award for being able to think at all.

She put a slice of the banana bread on a small white plate, then pinched off a piece and brought it to her lips. She took a bite, her eyes closing briefly. "This is awesome."

He watched her walk to the couch, set her coffee on the end table and then sit down with the plate on her lap. His gaze went to the curves of her calves, her slim ankles, the bright red toenails.

"I think I'll go take that shower now," he said abruptly, and this time he avoided her. Headed straight for the bathroom door. Before she got a load of his rising temperature.

DAKOTA WOLFED DOWN the rest of the banana bread and then got another piece. When depressed she didn't eat, but when she was nervous? Look out.

Was she crazy staying here with him? She could've been on a flight home already. She should have been at the office an hour ago. Never had she missed a single Saturday. Everyone knew that. Where would they think she was? There'd be questions. And stares. And…

She looked around for a clock but couldn't find one. Her watch was on the nightstand, but it didn't matter really. She'd call the concierge and find out when the next flight to New York was leaving.

She hesitated, recalled the way Tony's pecs swelled with muscle, the way the black hair got thicker as it neared his waistband. She wanted to explore every inch of him. Discover his muscular thighs. He was a laborer. Used every muscle in his body. Panicked, she searched for the phone. Why had he stopped her last night? It would have been so much easier when she was pretending to be drunk.

God, she was a coward. But she'd hate herself either way. Better not to have to face Cody at work. Would he have questioned her parents and got them concerned?

The phone rang just as she reached for it.

"Hey." It was Dallas.

"Where are you?"

"Still in the city."

"You're kidding."

"Nope. How's it going?" Dallas asked.

"Tony registered us under your names. But as far as I know, Tom hasn't tried to pull anything."

"Good. I think his wife may have reeled him in. Serena's pretty tired of his pranks."

"Oh, well, it's about time." Where had the disappointment come from? She'd already decided to leave. "No need for us to stay then."

"Dakota."

"What?"

"Don't be a chicken."

"What are you talking about?" She couldn't mean Tony. Dallas knew better. The lengthening silence told her otherwise. "Dal-las? What have you done?"

"Nothing."

"Tom wasn't going to sabotage you at all…was he?"

"Look, Dakota—"

"I've never interfered in your life."

"I'm not interfering. I asked you for a favor. You could've said no."

Dakota drew in a breath. She couldn't argue that point.

"I've gotta go," Dallas blurted. "We leave this afternoon for Budapest. We're taking one of those fourteen-day riverboat cruises to Amsterdam."

"Wow! Fourteen days?" Dakota didn't want to fight with her sister. Especially not before she traveled. The old childhood fear that something bad might happen while away had turned into a persistent superstition.

"Yep, after haggling with Mom over the wedding plans, a nice long vacation is exactly what we need."

She couldn't imagine being away from the office that long. It would be horribly nerve-racking. "Well, you guys have fun."

"We will. You, too. Cut loose, okay? No one's looking over your shoulder. And you couldn't find a better guy than Tony." Dallas abruptly hung up.

Dakota smiled wryly as she replaced the receiver. Look who was being chicken now. Sighing, she checked the pareu knot, although it was so short, calling it a pareu was stretching it. She could tie the cover-up around her waist, which was probably how it was meant to be worn, but of course that would cause another problem.

Maybe when they went to the beach, with all that sunshine and clean ocean air, she'd feel better. At least she wouldn't feel so exposed on a beach with other half-dressed people.

She wandered to the sliding glass door, which was still draped, odd considering they had an ocean view. No one's looking over your shoulder, Dallas had said. The weekend, the situation, it was all totally perfect. If she could have e-mailed the gang at Eve's Apple, they would have told her to go for it. Run, don't walk. This is what she wanted. She'd told them so just a couple of nights ago. So why the hell was she vacillating?

She found the cord for the drapes and pulled them open.

"Was that the phone?"

She heard Tony come up behind her but she just stared outside. At a dark sky, a gray turbulent ocean and the balcony wet from a recent rain.

"What are you looking at?" He stood beside her, smelling of soap and the croissant he'd brought with him. To her dismay, he was also wearing a T-shirt. But at least he'd had the courtesy to wear shorts, a little too long for her to get a look at his thighs but he had great calves.

She raised her brows at him. "What happened to the blue skies and sunshine?"

"Oh, that." He took a bite of the croissant. When he finished chewing, he said, "You have to believe, Dakota, have faith that everything will turn out all right."

"What kind of nonsense is that?"

"Nonsense?" He snorted, and then pointed outside. "Look over there."

"What am I looking at?"

"See that patch of blue?"

"Yes." She had no idea where he was going with this. But she loved just hearing his voice. Deep and soothing, sexy yet friendly. Maybe the playful friendliness was what made him sexy. She didn't know but she wasn't going to analyze further.

"You had faith and it's paying off."

"You're nuts."

He smiled, ate the last bite of his croissant and then took her by the hand. "And you're beautiful."

"Stop it."

He tugged her closer. "Like you haven't heard that a thousand times."

She sighed, disappointed. She really didn't want him to be like the other guys. The ones who couldn't see past the package. She'd outscored all of them in law school but it never mattered. "Is that why you're here with me?"

"Partly."

"What's the other part?"

He frowned thoughtfully for a moment while doing those little circles on the inside of her wrist again. "I'm thinking it might be because you play hard to get."

Pretty damn honest of him. "I never played hard to get. Did you ever think I just wasn't interested?"

"Nope."

That startled a laugh out of her. "Are you always this sure of yourself?"

"If I'm not, no one else will be." He ran his hand up her arm. "Want to hear part three?"

"Ah, there's more." She tried to stay cool when he grazed her shoulder and then cupped the side of her neck.

"I know a little about you from Dallas. Now, don't get your knickers in a twist," he said, when her mouth opened in protest. "It wasn't as if she was talking about you specifically. She was talking about herself and you just entered into the conversation."

"How?"

He smiled, massaged the back of her neck. "She didn't tell me you had a temper."

"I don't."

"The eyes don't lie."

She gave him a sugary smile, and said, "Can you guess what they're telling you now?"

"Ouch."

She laughed. She couldn't help herself. Although the fact that he was giving her the best neck rub ever certainly went a long way toward penance.

"As I was saying, part three, even though you're built like a—" At the lift of her eyebrows he paused. "Like a, um—"

"You don't have to stop rubbing my neck while you think."

He nodded and went back to work, his dark brows solemnly drawn together as if he had to decide the fate of the world. He'd missed a tiny spot shaving, right where his skin creased when he smiled. Which he did a lot. She liked that. "Okay, like a goddess," he said looking to her as if for approval.

"Oh, brother." She rolled her eyes.

"You like 'every guy's fantasy' better?"

Heat stung her cheeks and she moved away from him. "Would you stop."

"Hey, wait, there's more." He caught her hand and pulled her against him. She held her breath when his arm slid around her waist, forcing them to melt together. "Despite the fact that you're beautiful and could probably get anything you want, you have a serious career that you've worked hard for. And you took the time to help Nancy and Trudie and the rest of the ladies get Capshaw's attention."

"I really didn't do much."

"The harassment stopped. You did good. Get over it."

She gave him a wry smile. It was the best she could do considering how sensitive her breasts were, how achingly hard her nipples had become crushed against his chest.

His gaze lowered to her lips, and then he dipped his head and touched her mouth with his. Softly. A whisper of a touch, while his hands explored her back, followed the curve of her spine and cupped her bottom. She moved against him, felt his hardness growing, exciting her. Empowering her. Making her bolder.

She ran her tongue across his lips and then drew his lower one into her mouth. He let her take the lead, nibbling, tasting, exploring the inside of his mouth. Tension radiated from his body, fed her own and she fought the urge to back off. Slink to the corner. Run back to her safe, well-ordered life.

What was wrong with her? Had it really been that

long since she'd been with anyone? It wasn't as if Tony was a threat.

He must have sensed her withdrawal because he leaned back far enough to look at her. "Hey."

"Hey."

He touched the side of her cheek with the back of his finger, yet giving her some space. "Did you notice how much blue sky is showing now?"

She gave him a weak smile. "The sun's been out a couple of times, too."

"Is this where I tell you I told you so?"

"A couple of times does not a sunny day make."

He mockingly put a hand to his chest. "She's poetic, too. I think I'm in love."

She gave him a playful shove and felt his hard chest beneath her palms. Getting all heated again, she snuck a look and saw that he was still aroused. Now it was difficult to look away. Difficult to think about anything but dragging him to bed. She doubted he'd mind. And wasn't that why she was here?

"Look at that." He pointed at two couples in swimsuits, carrying snorkels, and walking along the shoreline. "Fellow believers."

Between two fluffy white clouds, the sun peeked out, so bright this time that Dakota had to squint to look up at the sky. It was definitely clearing up. Even the ocean was turning from gray to a pretty bluish-green. Several more people emerged from the bungalows close to the water, all of them in swimsuits and carrying towels.

"Maybe we should take advantage of the beach

while the sun's out," she said, expecting him to balk, to grab her and kiss her and convince her to crawl back into that nice big soft bed with him. Yeah, like she needed her arm twisted.

"Good idea." He took a step back. "I'll go put on my trunks."

She shrugged, trying not to show her disappointment. "After I slip on a pair of sandals I'll be ready."

He took a few more steps backward, his gaze taking her in, devouring her as if she were a hot fudge sundae. "I can't wait for you to baptize that suit."

"You're going to wait a long time. I can't swim."

"Excellent. I'll teach you."

Laughing and shaking her head, she pointed to the bathroom. "Go."

"Can't wait to get me in the water, huh?"

"I'm so embarrassed you guessed."

He winked and disappeared.

She couldn't stop smiling. She'd lied. Of course she could swim. In fact, she'd been ranked number two on her college swim team. But if he wanted to teach her, hey, who was she to argue.

6

WELL, NOW HE KNEW. Tony grinned to himself as he hauled two lounge chairs from the attendant's station near the pool, through the warm sand to a spot close to the water. Ms. Shea was hot for him, after all. Pretending she didn't know how to swim. Right. He knew damn well she'd been on her college swim team. It had somehow come up in conversation with Dallas once.

"Do you want an umbrella?" he asked her after he set his chair next to hers.

"I put on sunscreen."

"Yeah, but sometimes the sun and a hangover don't mix."

She wore sunglasses but he could tell she was glaring. "I don't have a hangover, nor am I as knowledgeable about them as you seem to be."

"Haven't had one myself since my college days. When are you going to take off that thing?"

She ignored the part about getting down to her bikini. "You went to college?"

"I'm wounded that you look so surprised." He kicked off his deck shoes and sand flew everywhere.

"I'm not surprised. Well, yeah, I am, but only because Dallas never said anything."

"So you asked about me?" He grinned at the long-suffering face she always made when he teased her. "I didn't finish. Too boring. I left halfway into my sophomore year."

He pulled off his T-shirt and folded it before stowing it with his towel under his chair. He probably should have put on sunscreen since he didn't work outside much anymore and his tan had faded. Truthfully, he was hoping they wouldn't be out long. He had far more interesting indoor activities planned.

Tony stretched out on the lounge chair and looked over at Dakota, anxious for her to unveil, his pulse racing like when he was a kid on Christmas morning and his parents finally brought out the big wrapped toy they always saved for last. But she was obviously in no hurry. She'd sat down but was still messing with the small bag of stuff she'd brought with her. Maybe she was even stalling.

He still didn't get it. How could she be so self-conscious? Was that why she dressed the way she did for work, or was that just part of the image she had of herself as an attorney? He understood the whole professional look, dress for success bit, but if the two times he saw her in work clothes were typical, then she carried it too far.

"Over there." Tony waited for her to look up and then motioned with his chin at a woman knee-deep in the water. "Now that's what they call itsy-bitsy."

"Oh, God."

"What?"

She just shook her head.

"Yours isn't that—" His heart thudded. "That's not a bad thing."

"I don't see you wearing a Speedo."

"Good point. But I'm just saying—"

He totally forgot what he was about to say when she got up, untied the knot at her breasts and let the wrap fall. Even at the risk of being rude, he couldn't take his eyes off her. He didn't know how she'd even gotten it on. A small yellow triangle took care of the bottom front and two triangles took care of the top. The rest was all her. Soft curves, pale skin and a flat belly she must have had to work hard for.

She quickly sat back down and with a glance over her shoulder said, "At least I don't know anyone here." She got comfortable, stretching out her long legs, her head tilted back so that her face got full sun, her back slightly arched.

He said nothing. With all the blood pooled in his groin, anything coming out of his mouth would probably sound juvenile. Other guys had noticed her, too, even ones with wives or girlfriends. And damned if he didn't get that same adolescent rush as he had when he'd trumped all the school jocks and taken Jackie Ricci, the homecoming queen, to the big dance. But that was seventeen years ago and he wasn't that same cocky kid anymore.

"Here comes a waiter. Do you want a drink?" he asked and she made a face.

She moistened her lips. "Maybe some plain orange juice."

Just watching the tip of her tongue took him to a place he shouldn't go. Not here. "Ah. Come on. Don't you want something with an umbrella in it?"

She sat up and looked in the direction of the approaching waiter. "I'll bet he'll put one in my orange juice."

Tony snorted. The guy would probably do anything she wanted, unless he was gay. Even sitting up her belly was flat. Her breasts weren't large but their size suited her slender body type perfectly. This time when he saw a couple of guys eyeing her it annoyed him.

"You ready for a swim?" His motives weren't entirely pure. A hard-on was starting to make him uncomfortable, and playing in the water invited all kinds of possibilities.

"We just sat down."

"I'll order our drinks, and they'll be waiting for us when we get out."

"You go on ahead and I'll wait for them." The wrap she'd left on the lounge chair, she now gathered to her sides as she settled back again, partially hiding her body.

He sighed and adjusted the towel to conceal the front of his trunks and stretched out again. He kind of liked it that she was modest. In his experience, women who looked as good as her went the other way. But jeez, she was beginning to cramp his style.

The waiter came and took their order and their room

number. Tony asked for juice, too. Didn't want alcohol to hinder his stamina. If he ever got a chance…

"Okay, let's go for a swim." She swung her legs over and her feet hit the sand. "I can't stand to watch a grown man sulk."

"Me?"

"Ouch, this sand is hot."

"Race you."

One second a challenging look, the next she was gone. Headed for the water. Man, she was fast. He didn't catch up until she was thigh deep, the gentle waves lapping against her and turning to foam like white frosting on a bluish green cake.

She laughed as he plodded his way to her, and he resisted the urge to splash her in the face. Dakota, on the other hand, had no such self-control. She got him first. Taking him totally by surprise.

He wiped his face. "Oh, it's like that, is it?"

Giggling like a little girl, she backed up. "Truce. Let's call a truce."

"Before I get even?"

"Come on. I said, truce."

"Tough." He advanced on her.

She turned and dove toward deeper water. Her strokes were clean and she moved at an impressive speed. He followed, and he was a pretty good swimmer himself, but not that good. Finally, he gave up and treaded water, waiting for her to come back.

She took her time, alternating with a backstroke, gracefully cutting through the water. When she finally glided toward him, he was beat just from trying to stay afloat.

"Hey, show-off." He started paddling backward toward the beach. "Thought you couldn't swim."

She grinned. "I may not have told the truth about that," she said and swam past him.

He flipped over and swam the rest of the way, too, staying fairly close on her tail. He'd probably end up having a heart attack but no way was he letting her leave him behind.

They got to the shore and although she wasn't out of breath, she'd obviously exerted herself. Him, he was gonna crawl to his lounge chair and slip into a coma.

"You were right. That felt terrific." She picked up her towel and wiped her face and then drew the towel down her arms and legs, across her chest.

Exhilarated from her swim, she didn't seem self-conscious now or maybe she was just too distracted to notice that a number of people were staring. Both men and women. Probably wondering if she were a model or an actress they should recognize.

She was really that stunning, and he realized that he wasn't that tired, after all. Sighing, he got back into position on the lounge chair, the towel again hiding his stubborn cock.

The waiter had left their glasses of juice on a small tray attached to their armrests. It took Tony two gulps to drain his, the icy coldness welcome as he baked under the hot sun. Dakota sipped hers, her eyes closed, before slipping her sunglasses on and then leaning back on her elbows.

Part of her left breast slipped out of the side of her top, just a small strip but enough to stir his imagination. Damn, he tried not to look. Sucked some ice out of his glass and chewed it instead. Tried to forget that her nipples stuck out, pushing against the wet top.

"Tony?"

"Yeah?"

"Are you okay?"

"Fine. Why?"

"It sounded like you were groaning."

He crunched down on the ice. "Nah, I was just clearing my throat."

"Okay." Then she stretched her arms over her head. "Can you believe this warm breeze? I think it was close to fifty when we left New York."

"Yeah, but look at those dark clouds headed our way."

She looked out at the horizon and then her lips curved in a teasing smile. "What happened to having faith?"

Getting rid of the hard-on he was having trouble with blew faith to the back of the line. "Touché, but I still think we should head inside."

"Let's stay just a little longer."

"You wanna see me sulk again?"

Her smile broadened. "I'll close my eyes."

"Tough broad, aren't you?"

"Hey, I resent that sexist remark."

"It's not sexist. It's just a—it's not sexist."

Turning toward the sun again, she huffed. "I suggest you think about it."

"With that tone, you should've been a school teacher." She already dressed like one, but he didn't mention that.

She started to say something but a red Frisbee landed in Tony's lap, and he grunted, cutting her off. The aim couldn't have been better. Damn good thing his arousal was on the downswing.

She bolted up. "Are you okay?"

"No."

A redheaded kid, early teens, ran up to them. "I'm sorry, mister. The wind caught it."

"No problem. Here you go." He tossed it back. "With that breeze picking up you should probably head further down the beach where it isn't crowded."

"Yeah, I guess. Sorry again." Walking backward in the soft sand, the kid almost stumbled over another couple. "Sorry," he said to them and ran.

"It's getting dangerous out here. I'm telling you, we'd better go in." He shifted and winced. The Frisbee had left its mark.

"You really did get hurt." She took off her sunglasses to regard him with concerned eyes.

"Nah, it's okay." Of course he may never have kids…

"Want me to kiss it and make it better?"

At a loss for words he stared at her. Did she have any idea what she'd just said?

"Oops." Laughing, she covered her mouth. The mischievous sparkle in her eyes said her words hadn't been innocent.

Man, was she hard to figure. "You're making me crazy, you know that?"

"Then my work here is done." She slid her sunglasses back up her nose, and returned to sun worshiping.

"Dakota?"

"Hmm?" She turned to him without raising her head.

"I wanna ask you something. If you don't wanna answer, I'm sure you'll tell me to shove it."

"Count on it."

He smiled. "Why do you dress so conservatively?"

Her lips tightened. "I'm an attorney. You want me to dress like a stripper?"

"Now see, there you go," he said, shaking his head. "Getting all defensive for nothing."

"Well, did I criticize how you dress?"

"I'm not criticizing." It was getting harder to keep the impatience out of his voice. "I'm curious because it's almost like you purposely try to look plain." He wanted to say frumpy but thought better of it.

"I think I look professional."

"Let's say you'd packed your own bag for this trip, what would you have brought?"

"A one-piece swimsuit because it's much more practical for swimming, and some shorts and maybe—" She sighed. "Why is this important?"

"Because you don't seem like a prude but you dress like one, and I'm trying to figure you out."

She sighed again and briefly closed her eyes before rolling over onto her side and supporting her head with her hand. The weight of her right breast at that angle kind of rolled partway out of her top and messed with his concentration.

She pushed her sunglasses up on her head and looked at him with frank eyes. "Mother always made Dallas and I dress demurely. Even as little girls, she wouldn't dress us in anything cutesy. So you can imagine how strict she was with us when we were teenagers. The whole reason being, any attention we received would be for our intellect or accomplishments and not our looks."

"Wow! Good intention, I guess." But he didn't get it. "Your mom's a good-looking woman herself, she must have had—" He stopped at the sudden wariness in her expression that told him the subject of her mother was closed.

Instead, he let silence stretch while he thought about Dallas and how she'd been affected. She talked about family stuff and vented about her demanding mother sometimes, but she never mentioned anything about being told how to dress.

And because she'd worked in construction with him, she'd worn jeans and T-shirts like the rest of them. Even when they'd gone for a drink after work, she changed to clean jeans and another T-shirt, totally in line with the bars they went to. But then, too, she had that short modeling career. Rebellion maybe?

Almost as if she'd read his mind, Dakota finally broke the silence and said, "Like Dallas I rebelled in college, too. I didn't want to model or anything like that. I started wearing short skirts, tight jeans and skimpy tops. Nothing horrible, I dressed just like all the other girls. And I found Mother was right." Dakota paused, visibly swallowed. "That wasn't the kind of attention I wanted."

There was more to it. A whole lot more, judging by the way she'd tensed. "Anything you want to talk about?"

"No."

"Okay. How about them Yankees?"

"They play basketball, right?"

"Do you have any idea how sacrilegious that is?"

"Football?"

"I hope you're kidding."

She laughed. "I bet I've been to more Yankee games than you have."

"No way."

"Care to make a wager?"

Either she had one hell of a poker face, or she'd told the truth. Didn't matter. He could keep staring at her all day. Her cheeks were starting to get a little pink from the sun and her gray eyes picked up the blue of the ocean and sky. Her skin would be salty from their swim and he wanted to lick it. Start from her lips and then head down to those silky-looking thighs.

She smiled. "I really do like baseball."

"No way."

"You need to work on your vocabulary."

"Your dad a fan?"

"Somewhat, but my brother is rabid over the sport."

"Cody?"

"I only have one brother," she said dryly.

"He doesn't seem the type."

"He played Little League and then some in high school, which my mother thought was a complete waste of time. But my father insisted it would be good for him and it turned out he liked it."

"Interesting." He couldn't imagine Cody Shea getting dirty. Not even as a kid.

She gave him a smug smile. "Thought you had us all figured out, didn't you?"

"Yeah, kind of."

She gave him a thoughtful look. "You're racking up points for honesty, by the way."

"Yeah? Like frequent flyer miles? After so many I get a free ride."

She bit her lip, obviously trying to hide a smile, and shook her head in mock disapproval.

"Am I right?" Trying to look affronted, he reared his head back. "You don't think I meant—Ms. Shea you surprise me."

"Tony, I have to say you are unique."

"Damn right I am."

"Okay, enough of that, your turn to tell me something."

"What kind of something?"

"About yourself."

He shrugged. "No skeletons in my closet. I had a boring childhood. My pop runs an auto body shop he inherited from his pop, and my mom stayed at home to raise us kids. Two brothers, one sister, a cousin I consider a sister because she grew up with us."

"Are they older, younger?"

He had no idea why that mattered but he answered, "I have one brother older than me."

"Are they married? Do you have nieces and nephews?"

"Everyone but my baby sister is married and they all have a bushel of kids. I can hardly keep the names straight." He lied. He knew each and every one of those rascals, and he hadn't missed a single silly birthday party.

"Do they all live in New York?"

"My younger brother just moved to Atlanta to help my grandfather with his carpet business. My mom comes from Georgia. All that side of the family is still there."

"That's so interesting. How did they meet?"

"She was a tourist. First day in the city a cab driver scared the hell out of her, so she rented a car."

Dakota winced. "Oops."

"Yep. He towed her to the shop the next day. You know the rest."

"A vacation romance that lasted. How about that?" She picked up her glass of orange juice and took the last sip. "How about you? Any particular reason you haven't gotten married?"

"Got a good pair of running shoes."

"Ah." She smiled and tipped the glass to get the last ice cube.

Mesmerized, he stared at the slender curve of her neck, at her well-defined jaw, at the small point of her chin, at her lips, the kind he liked, slightly turned up at the corners. He didn't know many women who were prettier when you got up close.

She sucked on the ice, and he even liked watching her throat work. How sick was that?

"Tony?"

He met her eyes, sleepy and sexy, and man, he had to reach for the towel again. "Yeah?"

"When are we having lunch?" she asked around a yawn.

Great. He was thinking about sex, and she was thinking about food. "Tell me something first…" He kept his eyes on her as she shifted her position, her cleavage deep, and wondered if she was torturing him on purpose. "You asked why I'm here with you. I told you. Your turn."

She lifted one shoulder. "For the sex."

7

DAKOTA KNEW HOW to keep a straight face. She did it in court all the time. But she almost lost it watching Tony's jaw drop. Though it started working again soon enough.

"Now you tell me. After we get out of the water?"

She laughed, the sound shaky, thinking about what she'd just said. Thinking about the bulge he was trying to hide. "We're on a beach. Lots of people. Kind of a deterrent, don't you think?"

"Now you expect me to think."

"Poor baby." She was glad she had sunglasses to hide behind as she rolled onto her back again. He had an amazing chest. Just the right amount of muscle defining his pecs and abs and shoulders, unlike some of the guys at the gym who pumped up until they practically had no neck.

"Is it getting hot, I mean like scorching out here, or is it me?"

She turned to him again, and said, "Race you." And then jumped up and threw off her sunglass before he could say a word.

He was a lot quicker getting to the water this time,

splashing her warm dry back as he ran up behind her. Before she could dive in, he grabbed her around the waist and they both went down laughing.

When she tried to right herself, she found her leg wedged between his thighs, rubbing him intimately with each kick. Good thing the water retarded the impact.

He grabbed her ankle. "Between you and the Frisbee, I'm gonna be out of commission for a year."

"Sorry."

"You could sound like you mean it."

She'd gotten the giggles, which sometimes happened when she got nervous. She'd actually admitted she was here for the sex. The salt air must have rusted her brain. But so what? That is what she wanted. So did he. That was obvious.

She pressed her lips together, cleared her throat and then got a false start. She tried again, and this time without laughing, she said, "I really am sorry."

He grinned, his teeth really white against his tanned face, and the direct sun bringing out some golden flecks in his brown eyes. "Prove it and you're forgiven."

"You'll have to let go of my ankle first."

"Swear you won't swim away."

"I promise."

"Okay." He loosened his hold. "I'm trusting you now," he said before totally releasing her.

"And to show you that trust wasn't misplaced..." She slid her hands up his chest, feeling his hard nipples beneath her palm, and then wound her arms around his neck.

Just as their lips met a wave hit them and they stumbled apart. Tony caught her and they both swung their gazes out to sea to fend off any more surprises. No large swells in sight but the water had definitely gotten choppy as the clouds headed inland.

Tony pulled her close again. The water hit them at chest level so when his hands ran down her back to cup her bottom she moved against him without fear that someone could see them. The funny thing was, she wasn't all that concerned anyway. This whole thing was so not her but it felt incredibly free and exhilarating to be here with Tony enjoying the freedom of doing whatever she pleased. Without censure. Without worrying that one little mistake could ruin her future.

"Look, the clouds are chasing people away," Tony said with a jut of his chin toward the beach.

She briefly glanced that way. Only a few sunbathers remained and some of them were packing up. "Ah, that just breaks my heart."

With both hands, he gently squeezed her backside. And when he slipped his fingers inside the elastic, her entire body thrummed with anticipation.

"Of course we could always go back to the suite." He nuzzled the side of her neck, and she closed her eyes.

"No, let's stay awhile."

"You're the boss."

"I like the sound of that." She shivered when he nipped an especially sensitive spot.

"Sure you don't want to go in?"

She shook her head. She'd never admit what a high this brief walk on the wild side was. He wouldn't understand. This was nothing for a guy like him.

"Here comes another wave. Not too big, but brace yourself." He ran his hands back up, encircling her with his arms and turning so that he received the brunt of the force.

She hid her face against his chest and tasted the salt on his skin. He jerked as her tongue got close to his nipple. Laughing, she looked up at him. "Ticklish?"

"No. You?"

It happened so fast she didn't know how he got his finger inside the elastic between her thighs. Dakota spread her legs a little farther apart. He found what he wanted and probed deeper, rubbing gently yet firmly, until tingling warmth surged through her blood.

She couldn't quite look at him. So she closed her eyes and tried not to claw his chest, tensing when he found the perfect spot to make her melt like warmed honey. She lowered one hand and explored the front of his trunks. He was hard, considering they were chest high in water that was starting to make her own skin shrivel.

Another wave knocked them off course, not a big one, but enough to dislodge his finger, and force her to cling to him with both hands. He gave a wry chuckle and brought his hand up slowly, as if memorizing her body. Finally, he held her by her upper arms.

His mouth curved in a smile that was different

than normal. Or maybe it was his eyes that were different, black almost and so full of desire it made her tremble with want. "Now are you ready to go inside?"

"I am so ready." Her voice came out a whisper barely intelligible above the crash of waves around them. "I'm ready," she repeated, but by the look in his eyes, he'd already gotten the message.

"WHO GETS THE SHOWER first?"

"You're kidding." Tony barely got the door of their suite closed when he took the beach bag out of her hands and dropped it on the floor. "I hope."

"Um, well…" Dakota wished she knew what she'd said that was so wrong.

"I have every intention of washing this very soft, very delectable back," he said, drawing her close and hungrily kissing the side of her neck.

"I see." She let her head drop back. Showering together seemed so intimate for the first time. She thought about what they'd just done in the ocean with a dozen people still on the beach and a giggle threatened to escape. "That makes your back fair game."

Tony chuckled against her throat. "Baby, any part of me you want, it's yours."

She kicked off her sandals. "That's quite an offer."

He kicked off one deck shoe. "I hope you take me up on it." He had trouble with the other one, and taking a small hop, he muttered a curse.

Dakota laughed and offered her shoulder. "Here, hold on to me."

"That's what got me in trouble in the first place."

He cupped her shoulder with one hand and used his other to loosen the shoe.

Looking down, she caught a glimpse of the front of his trunks, and understood what might have thrown him off balance. She swallowed and clutched his arm. Nothing but lean hard muscle. Not an ounce of spare flesh marred his taut belly. And it was all hers for the taking.

Tony got rid of the shoe and they left everything right there in front of the door, slowing making their way toward the bedroom. He untied her pareu, but held on to both ends drawing her along with him, kissing her as he walked backward, oblivious to the table he nearly tripped over, her laughing and the door frame he bumped into.

He pulled back to look at her. "I'm kissing you and you're laughing. How is this thing supposed to work if you take shots at my ego?"

She smiled. "What thing?"

"This thing." He lightly pinched her behind, and she yelped. "And this—"

She blocked his hand, not sure where he was headed, not sure if she really wanted him to stop. "No, I get it."

"You sure?" He bit her lower lip.

"Um, give me a minute."

"Just one." He reached behind her and pulled free the strings of her top before she knew it. Gasping, she caught the front before it fell, cupping a hand over each breast. He smiled, covering her hands with his. "Only looking for something to occupy myself while I wait."

She hesitated, and then he stroked the backs of her hands, and she loosened her grip and let the bikini top fall to the floor. He moved back, his gaze lowering to her bare breasts, his nostrils flaring slightly and his eyes as black as midnight.

"Dakota." He gave a slight shake of his head, and exhaled.

"What's wrong?" She shrank back a little, wanting to cover herself, wanting to replay the last ten seconds.

"Nothing." His laugh came out shaky. "You're just so damn beautiful."

She let out a breath she hadn't realized she'd been holding, and tentatively reached out a hand and put it flat against his chest. "So are you."

"Hey, think up your own lines." He seemed genuinely embarrassed, which was totally unexpected. Kind of fun, she thought. "You have a perfect man's body—broad shoulders, muscled but not too much—"

"Would you shut up?" He gave her no choice by kissing her hard and cupping her breasts with his slightly rough palms, kneading gently, grazing her hardened nipples, just enough to make her insane.

Lowering his head, he took one into his mouth, sucking, nibbling lightly, the sensation so sweetly satisfying that she moaned softly. Then he took the other nipple into his mouth, using the pads of his thumb and forefinger to console the one he'd abandoned.

Her nails dug into his shoulders. She flinched at what she'd done. He didn't seem to notice. Tony had gotten down on one knee, his hands bracketing her waist as his mouth moved lower, laving her navel, and then taking the bikini elastic between his teeth.

"Hey." She pushed her fingers through his hair and fisted the thick dark strands. "Shower first, remember?"

"Hmm?" He didn't stop. His tongue kept doing wicked things to her skin, and her resolve.

"Tony?"

He looked up, his lips moist, his eyes glazed.

"Shower?"

"Right." He bowed his head again, gave her a quick nip, and then slowly got to his feet, stopping to swirl his tongue around each nipple.

She wasn't so anxious to jump in the shower as she was to see him naked. His blue bathing suit was covering all the important parts and she'd felt enough of his firm, full ass to make her a little impatient. And that wasn't even the main event.

Thinking about it, her composure slipped and she roughly jerked him up. He looked at her, startled, but she kissed him, and then took him by the hand and headed for the bathroom.

She adjusted the water to the right temperature while he stripped off his trunks. She turned around and held her breath. He wore nothing but a tan and budding hard-on.

"Your turn," he said, his gaze going to her breasts, lingering, and then finally to her bikini bottom.

Boy, she'd screwed that up. She should've made him ready the shower. She'd always hated undressing in front of anyone. Way too awkward, even though there wasn't much to take off.

She hooked her thumbs on either side and slid the tiny yellow bottom to her ankles and sure enough, had some trouble stepping out of it. She grabbed the towel bar for support and swore to herself that if he was laughing, she'd sock him. After untangling the bottom from her left foot, she straightened.

He wasn't laughing. His arousal was at full bloom, thick and ready, and she couldn't help but stare. She tried to think of something clever to say. She couldn't even come up with anything stupid. Her brain totally shut down.

Her only consolation was that he seemed just as powerless. He stared back, his gaze so primal and hungry it sent an electric shock down her spine.

She moistened her parched lips and spoke first. "The water is ready."

He grinned. "Me, too."

Her laugh came out nervous. One of them had to make a move. Her feet didn't seem to be cooperating. "I think there's another bar of soap on the vanity."

He turned around. "Got it."

God, he had a great ass. She raised her gaze just as he looked back at her. He gestured for her to go first, and she smiled to herself. That was one for him. She did, and quickly got into the large glass enclosed shower to stand directly under the spray of warm water. He slipped in right behind her, bringing his arms around her middle and pulling her back against his chest.

Her ass pressed against his arousal and when his hands came up to cup her breasts she was certain he could feel her heart pounding so hard and so fast that she didn't think she'd survive. He toyed with each nipple, rubbing and lightly pinching and then one of his hands moved down her belly. She sucked in a breath and slowly moved her hips, her ass taunting his long hard penis.

He groaned, his hand slackening on her breast, and then she felt him shudder. He took her by the shoulders and turned her around to face him. Cupping her face, he kissed her hard, slanting his mouth over hers, he delved in, leaving no virgin territory.

Horribly in need of air, they pulled apart to take a breath. Dakota laughed softly, her breathing still uneven. Wet strands of hair clung to her cheeks and he gently brushed them back, sinking his fingers in her hair and massaging her scalp.

Dakota let her head loll back briefly and then brought it forward before she got too relaxed, and smiled. "You have a thing for water, don't you?"

He grinned. "Seawater, pool water, showers, baths, it's all good when you're naked." He glanced down and muttered a mild oath.

"What's wrong?" She glanced down, too.

"Look what I've done to you." He gently touched the red area on her breast, and then his hand went to his jaw. "I should have shaved first."

"It's okay." She touched his face. It really wasn't too rough yet. "I have sensitive skin." Especially since it hadn't had any roughness on it for so long, but she didn't tell him that. "But I don't feel anything. Promise."

He gave her a look of mock horror, his eyes sparkling and crinkling at the corners. "You don't feel anything?"

She realized where he was going with this and tried to hide a grin. "Nothing," she said, all innocence.

"We'll have to fix that." He didn't hesitate and went straight for the juncture between her legs.

Evading him just in time, and grabbing the soap she said, "Turn around."

His mouth curved in a cocky smile. "Oh, baby, I like it when you give me orders."

"Well, then, do it." She'd make a lousy dominatrix. The urge to laugh was almost too strong.

"Be still my heart." He turned around and flattened his hands against the beige contoured tile.

For a moment she just stared, letting the water pelt her back. His cheeks indented on the sides as flesh molded muscle. With his arms raised, his pec muscles bunched and mounded. Sinew stretched across his powerful back, making him look impossibly broader.

How she wanted to run her palms over every inch of him. Feel every dip and bulge, even the rather long scar on the side of his thigh. She gingerly traced it with her finger.

He looked over his shoulder. "Happened at work about seven years ago. My own stupidity."

She kissed his back and then started soaping him, starting at his shoulders, and then reaching around to his chest. She felt his sharp intake of breath as she brought his nipples to life, and then traveled to his stomach. She stopped there, smiling to herself, knowing his anxiety was increasing. But so was hers, so who was she tormenting?

"Okay, you." He abruptly turned around, and produced a pink squishy bath sponge.

"Where did you get that?"

"Up here."

She followed his gaze to a small ledge that had been discreetly built into the tile. There were two more, housing a tube of bath gel and something she didn't recognize. She got closer and realized that was what was providing the herbal scent she'd smelled. "Wow, how cool is that? I totally missed it. How did you find them?"

He shrugged. "I did something similar in my shower. Only the nooks are bigger, almost the size of the tile and I put—" He smiled. "I'm not telling you any more. You'll see for yourself."

Dakota stiffened. See for herself? She would never see the inside of his apartment. Didn't he understand? They wouldn't see each other once they got back to the city. This was a one-time thing. A brief escape from reality. When they got back, it was over.

She was so swamped with work that she spent most of her time at the office. A social life wasn't optional. Not at this point in her career. Anyway, they'd have no reason to see each other again. Except for sex maybe. But that was way too close to home. She couldn't take that risk.

Tony frowned. "What's wrong?"

"Nothing." She shook her head. "Actually, I'm feeling a little waterlogged."

He looked at his palms. The skin on the pads of his fingers had shriveled. "Yeah, I'm feeling like a prune myself. Let's hurry up and get out of here. I think horizontal might be nice for a change."

She accepted his kiss without the enthusiasm she had earlier. Fortunately, he didn't notice. They finished washing without playing around. Any move he made she playfully blocked. But she wasn't feeling so playful anymore. Not until they talked. Not until she was certain he understood where she was coming from. Not until she presented the terms of their brief relationship.

8

After she'd dried off, Dakota reached for the white hotel robe. While slipping into it, she caught Tony's confused look. He was still naked, although not as aroused. He looked so good she wanted to throw away caution. Forget the short speech she'd been preparing in her head. But she knew better. That would be incredibly foolish. Better to spell out the ground rules first.

"There's another robe behind the bathroom door," she said. "I'll get it for you."

He got hold of her wrist. "I was thinking naked would be best."

"I'm thirsty. Let's have something to drink first. Otis said the fridge is stocked with beer." Headed toward the parlor, she said over her shoulder, "But feel free to stay naked."

She kept going, trying to ignore the puzzled hurt in his eyes. He thought something was wrong. Of course that wasn't true, and the sooner they discussed the arrangement the sooner everything would be fine again.

She found a diet cola in the fridge and brought

it out along with his brand of domestic beer. By the time she got a glass and some ice for herself, he joined her, dressed in the matching robe. Frowning, he sat on one of the bar stools across from where she stood.

"What's wrong, Dakota?" he asked, taking the beer she offered, but setting it on the bar while he looked her in the eyes.

"Nothing." She popped the top of the can and started pouring the cola into the glass. "Seriously. Nothing. But I do want to talk."

"About?"

"Don't look so worried. It's no big deal." She set down the can and came around the bar to face him. She grabbed his lapels and pulled him toward her for a kiss.

He readily accommodated her, taking hold of her hips and pulling her between his legs. She tried to keep a level head, which wasn't easy knowing he wore nothing under the robe and only inches away was the mother lode. This wasn't at all how she wanted things to go.

Tony was a dangerous man. At least for her he was. He disturbed her mental equilibrium. Tempted her to be imprudent. Not good. Not good at all.

She broke the kiss. "The sooner we talk, the sooner we get back to the fun stuff."

"Uh-oh."

"What?"

"This sounds bad."

She stepped back and put her hands on her hips. His gaze immediately went to her chest and she realized the robe had fallen open, exposing one of her breasts. The longing on his face was almost her undoing.

Quickly turning away, she pulled herself together, and then took a deep cleansing breath.

"Okay, let's talk," he said, uncapping his beer bottle and taking a big gulp.

"Okay." She cleared her throat. "I realize this is a little late but I think we should establish some rules for the weekend."

His dark brows drew together in a frown. His hair was still wet and a thick lock fell across his forehead. He looked so adorable she could just eat him with a spoon.

"That's not quite accurate. We don't need rules now. That's what's great about being here. Away from Manhattan. Here nothing counts."

She smiled, but he didn't.

"That's a good thing, right?" She sighed when she got no reaction. "Here's the reality. When we get back to the city, work is going to be a bitch. I'm losing two days I hadn't anticipated. Even in the best of circumstances I don't have the kind of free time to grab a last-minute dinner or if you find cheap same-night theater tickets."

Realizing she'd begun her practiced pacing, like she did in court when she addressed a jury, she moved behind the bar and leaned over across from him. His face was an unreadable mask. And she was damn good at reading people.

She cleared her throat again. "I'm sure this is a relief for you. No expectations once we leave the island."

He didn't look relieved. He didn't look anything.

"Tony, do you understand what I'm saying?" They stared at each other for a long time, and she was tempted to point out his remark about good running shoes.

"Why do you feel the need to bring this up?" he asked finally, flatly.

"I just wanted to set the record straight. I'd think this talk might put you at ease."

"Oh. So this is for my benefit."

"For both of us." She sensed his anger, yet didn't understand it. "I'm not saying any of that affects us now. Maybe I didn't need to bring it up."

"I'm glad you did." He nodded pensively, his gaze straying out the glass doors before coming back to her. "Finished?"

"You're taking this totally wrong. Remember that I didn't have the benefit of preparing the night before this trip. Plus I wasn't exactly sober last night, if you recall." Panic needled her. "Not that I'm unhappy to be here."

He got up, without a word, leaving his half-full beer on the bar.

"The silent treatment doesn't help," she said when he headed toward the bedroom.

"I'll be right back." He didn't even turn around, or spare her a brief look.

She stared after him, angry, bewildered and a little sad. He just didn't understand. And she wasn't sure how to explain her situation. Her career had become increasingly demanding. So had her parents. She laughed humorlessly. Her brother, too. Everyone seemed to want a little piece of her and she didn't have anything left to give. To top off everything, it meant she was a miserable coward.

Not three minutes later he emerged from the bedroom. The moment she saw him wearing the blue-and-tan tropical shirt and khaki shorts, she knew she'd blown it. He had something in his hand and laid it on the bar in front of her. It was her airline ticket.

"The concierge should be able to help you get the next flight." Emotionless words and a shuttered face, and then he gave her a reluctant smile, full of weariness, disappointment and resignation. "Have a safe trip."

When he kissed her lightly on the cheek, he might as well have slapped her.

NORMALLY TONY APPRECIATED reggae music. Not now. Half the tables were taken, couples mostly, talking and laughing, some of them too loud. He wished the band would disappear and everyone would shut up. Though he was the idiot who had chosen a bar for him to wallow in misery. He could've walked the beach. But it was drizzling and he didn't feel like getting wet again.

Hell.

He probably couldn't splash his face again without thinking of Dakota. Naked. Water streaming down her incredible body. Her perfect pink nipples glistening with moisture. Hell, all he'd have to do was picture her in her office, behind her big important desk, doing whatever important things she did. That would cool him off real quick.

"You want another one of those?" the stocky bartender asked.

"Sure, why not?" Tony pushed the empty bottle toward him, and squinted at his name tag. Edward. He liked calling people by name and normally would have learned the bartender's name right off the bat. But a certain pain-in-the-ass woman had him in a tailspin.

"Thanks." Tony brought the new bottle to his lips.

"Sure you don't want a mug." Edward wiped his hands on the yellow towel he kept thrown over his shoulder. "I keep 'em nice and frosty."

"No, thank you." Tony snorted, and then muttered, "I left something pretty frosty upstairs."

The bartender chuckled, his black eyes sparkling as he leaned his short beefy forearms on the bar. "You have a problem, you talk to Uncle Eddie. He's heard everything."

"Me? Nah. No problem at all." This time he took a long drink of beer and then reached for a handful of pretzels from a wooden bowl sitting on the polished mahogany bar.

"You like nuts?" Eddie asked in a whisper. "I save them for my favorite customers." He brought out another bowl, this one with peanuts and cashews. After setting it in front of Tony, Eddie helped himself to some. "You don't look so good, buddy. You sure you don't wanna talk."

"That customer is trying to get your attention." Tony motioned with his chin toward the balding guy wearing a loud Hawaiian shirt and holding up an empty glass.

"Be right back." Eddie grabbed another handful of nuts and moved to the other end of the bar.

Tony hoped he'd stay there. Eddie seemed like a

nice enough guy, but sometimes—times like these especially—a person just wanted to be left alone. Amen. The guy was slick, bringing out the nuts, giving Tony that favorite customer crap. He didn't blame Eddie, bucking for a good tip. And Tony would give him one, if he left Tony the hell alone.

Chuckling, Tony took another pull of beer and then stared at his wet napkin.

His stomach growled and he went for the nuts. Tilting his head back, he dropped some into his mouth through an opening from his fist. Nice and salty. He dropped in a few more. No use saving room for lunch. Or dinner. After Dakota left, he'd probably fly back, too.

Damn her.

He sighed. Why'd she have to go and ruin the weekend? Everything was going so well, and then pow! He'd felt as if she'd hit him with a two-by-four upside the head.

To be fair, she was right about having been at a disadvantage last night. Dallas shouldn't have waited until Dakota had had so much to drink before she explained about the honeymoon decoy thing. And maybe when he'd seen how out of it she was, he shouldn't have let her get on the plane.

Still, none of that mattered. What she'd brought up in that annoying lawyer tone of hers had nothing to do with today. Or tomorrow. She was worried about what might happen when they got back. Like maybe he wasn't good enough to socialize with. That stung.

"Hi."

At the soft feminine voice he looked up, his heart thudding. He knew it wasn't Dakota's slightly husky timbre, so why the disappointment?

"This seat taken?" This unfamiliar woman was blond, petite and young. Real young. Like someone-should-card-her young.

"It's all yours."

She hiked a hip onto the bar stool beside him and then wriggled her way against the rattan back. Her already short dress rode up alarmingly high, which didn't seem to bother her.

"My name is Celine." She put out her hand. "Like the singer." She had one of those soft limp hand-shakes that he despised. But she was young. Maybe she'd learn that if you offer your hand you should act as if you mean it.

"My name's Tony. Like the tiger."

She giggled. Not the sexy throaty kind of giggle Dakota made in the surf. But an annoying girlish sound.

"Did you just make that up?" she asked.

"All by myself."

"Celine, your usual?" Eddie called to her from the other end of the bar.

She nodded and cocked her head toward Tony. "Give him one, too."

Tony held up a hand. "Nope. I've had enough, thanks."

"Oh." She sighed, her lips forming a disappointed pout. "Are you on vacation?"

"Sort of." Small talk wasn't his thing but he didn't want to be rude. "You?"

"Sort of." She grinned and then picked up the fruity-looking umbrella drink Eddie set down for her. "Although I practically live here. On the island, not the hotel."

"What is that?"

"A piña colada." She removed the pineapple wedge from the rim. "Want some?"

He glanced at Eddie, but he'd already moved on to another customer. Tony frowned at her. "Are you old enough to be drinking that?"

She giggled again, and he made a mental note not to encourage that sound anymore. Not that he'd said anything funny.

"I'm twenty-two," she said, leaning toward him far enough to show some lethal cleavage. "Totally legal."

"When did you get in, Celine?" Eddie joined them, taking the towel from over his shoulder and wiping down the area around their drinks.

"This morning. Daddy wanted to dock by yesterday afternoon but one of the deck hands got sick, and then we got caught in that rainstorm."

"You ought to show him your yacht," he said to her, and winked at Tony when she wasn't looking.

"Sure." She perked up. "Would you like to come see it?"

"Uh, well—"

Something brushed his right shoulder. He turned to find Dakota sliding into the bar stool on the other side of him.

"Hey." She had on a strappy red sundress, low cut, short and tight.

"Hey," he said back. "You're still here."

She nodded, and in a low voice asked, "Is that okay with you?"

He shrugged. "Not my call."

"Are you staying?"

"I don't know yet."

She sighed. "I know you're angry and I don't blame you." She moistened her lips. "I was wrong."

Eddie showed up. "Good afternoon, pretty lady, what can I get you?"

"I, um, I—" Her eyes filled with uncertainty, she looked at Tony and then darted a look at Celine.

"She'll have a white wine. Chardonnay," he added, by way of telling her she was welcome to stay.

"Thank you."

Tony really didn't want to stick around and talk here, but he didn't want to scare her off either. Better to scare off the other two. He turned back to Celine and smiled. "Excuse us. We're on our honeymoon."

The young woman's brows shot up. "Oh, sorry. I didn't know."

"No problem. You didn't do anything wrong." He couldn't wait to get a look at Dakota's face. Probably sitting there all prickly over his lying about the honeymoon part. Tough.

He slid her a look. Surprisingly, a smile tugged at her lips.

"Did you say you guys are on your honeymoon?" Eddie set down the chardonnay in front of Dakota. "For my favorite customers I have some very special champagne."

Dakota winced. "Um, thanks, but I think I'll have to pass on that. Too much at the wedding last night."

"Yeah, she had way too much. Dancing on the tables, the whole bit. I had to step in when she started to strip."

Everyone laughed, even the couple sitting at a nearby table.

She glared at him. "I did not."

"That's okay, honey." He squeezed her hand. "I know you don't remember and I shouldn't have brought it up."

She glanced around. "He's lying."

"She's right." Tony nodded condescendingly. "Yeah, I made it up."

Eddie gave him a you're-asking-for-it look, and shaking his head, ambled toward the other end of the bar.

Dakota's mouth tightened and then her lips slowly curved in a forced smile. "Okay, I guess I deserved that," she said softly.

Tony scoffed. "First of all, I wasn't taking jabs at you. Going for payback. I wouldn't do something that juvenile. Secondly, you need to lighten up. I was teasing. Couldn't you tell?"

"This was a mistake. You're hurt and angry and I should—"

He caught her hand before she got all the way off the stool. "I'm not hurt! Why would I be hurt? What irritated me was you're acting like a damn lawyer."

"I am a lawyer."

"Not upstairs in that bedroom you aren't."

She blushed and glanced to her left.

He was certain no one heard. He'd been careful to speak softly.

"Well, it was nice meeting you, Tony," Celine said from behind him. He'd forgotten about her sitting there.

"Same here."

"I've gotta go find my father." She smiled at Dakota. "Maybe I'll see you guys around."

After she was out of earshot, Dakota's gaze followed her. "Is she old enough to be in here?"

"Her?" He shrugged casually. "Sure."

"She looks so young."

"The older you get, the younger they start looking."

She turned to him with one brow lifted. "I get it. You're teasing, right? Ha. Ha."

"Don't be so touchy."

"I'm not," she said with a mischievous glint in her eyes. "Now if I were over thirty I might be a little sensitive."

"I wouldn't know." Close to thirty-four, he hadn't grown up yet so it didn't count.

"Right." She sipped her wine, and then picked a cashew out of the bowl.

"Hey, you have to ask me for those. I got them because I'm a special customer. Just ask Eddie."

"May I?"

She gave him such an oddly affectionate smile he got the sinking feeling he was about to get the let's be friends speech. "Knock yourself out."

He waited but she just scooped up a couple more nuts and put them in her mouth one at a time and chewed. Something he totally didn't get. How could anyone eat one nut at a time? "How old are you?"

She looked startled. "Where did that come from?"

"We were talking about age. It's not a stretch."

"I'm twenty-eight."

He let out a low whistle.

"What? Too old for you?" She glanced at Celine's vacated seat. "I notice you like them pretty young."

"Yeah, like twenty-eight is *so* old. I thought you were older."

Her eyes widened.

"Not because you look it. I did the math. College, law school, successful career, looking to be a judge already. All at twenty-eight. Pretty ambitious."

"To become a judge you have to look ahead and map out your career."

"Don't get defensive. I'm not criticizing you. Everyone should be able to live how they want."

She looked at him for a long moment, a sad smile on her lips as she switched her gaze to the napkin under her glass.

He couldn't help himself, he had to ask. "What?"

She sighed. "Some people think my parents have pushed me into a law career, that it's my father's ambition I become a judge and not mine. I think maybe even Dallas believes that. But it's not true. I loved law school. I loved learning so much about our justice system." She laughed. "I don't always appreciate the way it works. But I love it. I can't explain it."

"You don't have to. Not to me. I get it. I love what I do. I love working with my hands." He decided he wanted another beer after all and signaled for Eddie. "I just don't like working as many hours as you do."

"I don't always like it." She shook her head, a wistful expression on her face. "I have to. Having a father that's a prominent judge isn't easy. It doesn't mean I'll get a break. It means I'd better *really* measure up."

Eddie brought Tony's beer and while Dakota asked the bartender about one of the tropical drinks he'd prepared for someone else, Tony stared thoughtfully at her profile. He'd thought he understood, but he hadn't. Until now. Dakota *had* to work twice as hard— Being a Shea took its toll.

9

DAKOTA CHOSE a pretty pink fruity drink, minus the alcohol. Drinking hard liquor after wine was a bad idea. Besides, she had plans for tonight. Big plans that could hopefully last all night. And she needed her strength.

She felt the weight of Tony's stare, and purposely crossed one leg over the other, her red toenails peeking out of the sandals and pointing at him. That got his immediate attention. Thank goodness men were so easy.

"Have you eaten yet?" she asked, swinging her calf a little, watching him reluctantly drag his gaze away.

"Uh, no. Just pretzels and nuts."

"Would you like to have dinner with me?" The lack of a quick response made her stomach tighten. Her confidence vanished. Had she totally blown it? Here was this great guy who'd wanted nothing from her but a consensual weekend of fun.

Earlier, when she'd gotten on her high horse and started dictating terms, he could have gone along, agreed to anything just to get to the sex. But he'd stood up for his principles. He wasn't like so many of those guys in college and law school who couldn't see past her looks.

She cringed just thinking about how she must have sounded. As if he were only good enough for a weekend fling. But not good enough to be in her life. That he could never fit into her world. The sad part was, to her utter shame, the thought had crossed her mind. Not that he wasn't good enough, but that she'd be burdened trying to fit a square peg in a round hole. And that her career might suffer.

Revisiting the thought shamed her all over again. When had she become so damn arrogant? Tony was too full of fun and life and self-confidence. He wouldn't even be interested in her narrow, pathetic world. "I guess I should have asked if you're planning on staying," she said finally.

"I doubt I could get a flight out at this point."

"Oh."

"Not that I would." He smiled and winked. "I'd have to be crazy to give up our honeymoon."

Hope fluttered in her chest. "May I assume I'm forgiven?"

He gave her a heart-melting look and then leaned forward to kiss her briefly. "I'm glad you stayed."

"Me, too."

"No more talk about later. One day at a time. Okay?"

"Agreed."

"Now, about dinner?"

"There are three potential restaurants; casual, fancy and one with Indonesian food. You choose."

"Indonesian?"

She shrugged. "Go figure."

"There is another possibility." He picked up her hand and kissed the back, his eyes dark with meaning. "We could have room service."

"Even better. Good plan." She moved her leg so that her foot touched his calf, and then ran her big toe up as far as she could. "I like it."

His dark brows went up. "Except it's too early for dinner."

"True. Any ideas?"

He smiled. "One."

THE ELEVATOR DOORS OPENED and Tony let out a low growl. "Damn it."

"What?" She looked to see what had gotten him upset. One side of the double doors to their suite was open and parked in front of them was the maid's cart. "Oh. No way."

He held the elevator doors open and then followed her out to the corridor. "Maybe she's almost done. If not we'll kick her out."

"Nice."

"Would you like to invite her to stay for tea?"

She jabbed him with an elbow to the ribs, and he grunted. "Wise guys don't get laid," she whispered.

He laughed loud enough for the maid to hear and stick her head out.

A big smile lit her round brown face. "Come, come. I make ready." She motioned with her plump hand and then pushed the cart to give them room to squeeze by.

Dakota took the lead into the parlor. Something in the dining room caught her eye. On the table was a huge bouquet of red roses, white carnations and baby's breath sitting next to a silver bucket holding a bottle of champagne. Chocolates and petit fours arranged on a white lace doily topped a rattan tray.

"Wow, look."

Tony came up behind her and put a hand at the small of her back left bare by the sundress. She could feel his touch all the way to her thighs. She turned her face toward his and his gaze dropped to her mouth.

"Excuse me." Dressed in a crisp black-and-white uniform, the maid hurried by with folded cream-coloured towels, and headed for the bathroom.

Tony sighed, and then went straight for the chocolates.

"Is there a card?" Dakota asked.

"Screw the card. Check this out. White-chocolate covered macadamia nuts, English toffee, almond clusters... Oh, baby."

"You like chocolate. Just a wild guess." She plucked the small white envelope from the bouquet of flowers.

"Not to would be un-American."

"I thought that was mom and apple pie."

"Whatever." He selected one and bit into it.

She opened the envelope. "It's from Dallas and Eric. They wanted to thank us for doing this."

He chuckled. "Yeah, such a hardship."

The maid appeared, smiling, walking briskly from the bathroom. "Everything okay?"

"Everything is great. Thank you."

"I go now."

Dakota walked her to the door, and after she left, secured the dead bolt. She turned around to find Tony grinning at her. It was obvious what he was thinking. Too bad she didn't have a comeback because it was true. She was anxious to be alone with him.

He was munching on his second chocolate. "Dallas say anything else?"

Dakota shook her head, gazing at the flowers and champagne. "I wish they hadn't done this. This whole weekend is costing them a fortune already. Tom needs a swift kick in his butt."

"I know. But don't worry about it. I'm footing the bill."

"What?"

He shrugged. "No big deal. I haven't had a vacation in a long time."

She hesitated, careful not to hurt his feelings. The hotel was expensive. She knew that much for sure. And a suite? He had no idea. "Actually, I'd already planned on taking care of it. She is my sister."

"*Actually,*" he said with a smug smile. "It's already done."

"What do you mean?"

"I stopped at the front desk before I went to the bar. Gave them my charge card and had them transfer the cost."

"Oh." She wanted to ask if he'd seen the bill. If he knew what he was in for. On a construction worker's pay he thought he could take care of it?

Heck, she'd hate coughing up that much. But at least she could and still pay her rent. Yet how could she bring it up without hurting his feelings?

"And yes, don't worry, I can afford it. You want one of these?"

"I didn't—" She shut up. What more could she say without getting in trouble? "Anything milk chocolate." She went over to him, reminding herself she simply had to let it go. He was a big boy.

"Here." He put a piece of chocolate to her lips.

She bit into it and let the creamy smoothness coat her tongue. "Mmm, heaven."

"Give me a taste."

"Too late."

"I don't think so." With a hooked finger he brought her chin up. He kissed her gently at first, and then so greedily her head went back.

She laid her hands on his forearms, thinking she'd slow him down, but instead ran her palms up to mold his rounded biceps. When he put a hand on each side of her hips, the muscles hardened beneath her palms. Wanting his shirt off she went for the buttons. They slid out easily and his shirt hung open.

Smiling against her mouth, he tackled the straps that crossed over her breasts. They wouldn't be easy to unfasten, in fact she doubted he'd succeed, but she'd let him try while she explored the contours of his chest.

He finally gave up and released her. She wasn't so eager to abandon her exploration but he took hold of her wrists. "What do you say we go try that nice big bed in there?"

"I've already tried it. It's wonderful."

"Yeah, thanks, so was the couch."

"Poor baby."

"Fine. I don't want your sympathy. Just tell me how this damn dress works." He started walking her backward toward the bedroom.

She laughed. "It's like one of those puzzles. If you can figure it out you can have the prize inside."

"Ah. You mean the kind that makes me so nuts I tear and rip until I get what I want."

She stopped. "Don't you dare. This is a great dress."

"I agree. Are you going to wear it again?"

"Yes."

"When? Back home?"

She glared, annoyed with his goading. Although his shirt still hung open, and she knew damn well what that totally yummy chest felt like pressed against her breasts, and here they were wasting the afternoon. "Excuse me, but what happened to one day at a time?"

He put up his hands in surrender. "You're right. I concede."

She grabbed hold of the front of his shirt. "The hell with conceding. I want you to kiss me."

"Yeah?" He got up close, his warm lips brushing hers, and said, "Then take that damn dress off."

She made a ridiculous noise that sounded suspiciously like a giggle. She didn't care. Her concentration was directed at getting undressed. Before she even started she was halfway there. No bra. Only thing under the brief dress were uncomfortable thong panties, something with which she really wasn't happy and Dallas would hear about.

Tony got rid of his shirt and had his shorts off in concert with her throwing off the sundress. All their clothes astoundingly landed on the chair near the window. She pulled the bedspread back while Tony did his best to hinder her progress by trailing kisses down her back.

She'd barely gotten to the sheets when he urged her down onto the bed, stretching over her, kissing her mouth, her eyes, her throat. Shamelessly she ran her hands over his chest and shoulders, down his back, and then cupping his backside, squeezing the solid muscle, drowning in the sensation of his rock-hard penis rubbing her belly and the triangle of hair that absurdly felt as if it were on fire.

"Tony?" His name fell off her lips before she really knew what she wanted to say. When he pulled back to look at her, realization took hold. "I'm glad I'm here with you."

He smiled. "Me, too." He brushed the hair back from her face and then drew the pad of his thumb across her lower lip. "Me, too," he repeated, before lowering his mouth to her breast.

He caught her budded nipple lightly between his teeth and touched the tip with his tongue while he kneaded her other breast. She closed her eyes, amazed at the shivery sensation that controlled her body. She wanted to touch him, too, but she couldn't seem to get her arms to move.

When she finally overcame her lethargy and

summoned the strength to raise her right arm, he gently pushed it back down into the mattress. He kept her wrist captive, not in a scary way, but in a way that turned her on more than she could've imagined.

Selfishly she was glad. She wanted to just lie there and soak up all the delicious sensations that her body had been deprived of for too long. As well as she knew her own body, honed her own pleasures, taking care of herself didn't come close to the way Tony seemed to know exactly where and how to touch her. Knew how to push her to the brink, and then bring her back wanting more.

He took his time, laving her, discovering every curve, every crevice. This leisurely pace couldn't be easy for him. Not as incredibly hard as he was, his penis prodding her thighs, rubbing her belly as he moved over her.

Her impatience grew with the desire to touch him, and she broke free to run her palms up the side of his hips, and then down his taut backside. He moved against her, his arms shaking with restraint. Moisture formed at the tip of his penis and she could feel it on her belly, feel her own wetness between her thighs.

"Tony?"

He kissed her, the taste of rich chocolate still on his lips. He started slow, a soft brushing, a light nip, but the urgency increased and he parted her lips with his tongue, taking all she gave, taking what he wanted.

When he finally pulled back, his breathing was ragged, his voice hoarse. "Yeah?"

She stared blankly. "I forgot."

He chuckled and rolled to his side. After touching the tip of each nipple with his tongue, he settled back on his side, his head braced by his hand. His gaze swept her body and then rested on her face.

"Need a breather?" she asked sweetly.

"No, but I figure if I don't take a time-out, you'll need more than that."

"Aren't we cocky?" She reached down and ran two fingers along the underside of his penis, getting to the head and using her thumb to spread the moisture.

He briefly closed his eyes, muttered a mild curse and then maneuvered her hand away.

"Sorry, I forgot you needed a breather." She lay back, moving her hand to a spot right above her breasts.

His gaze followed her hand, watched as her fingers idly grazed a nipple. He took a deep shuddering breath, his chest rising and falling and begging her to touch him.

"You're beautiful," she whispered.

He met her eyes, his both surprised and amused.

"I mean it." She moved her hand to his chest, running her palm ever so lightly over his pecs, tracing the muscled slopes.

He chuckled, shaking his head, and by his self-conscious expression she realized she'd embarrassed him.

"The guys at my gym would kill to look like this." She ran her hand down his flat belly. Touched his arousal, watching her finger circle the head, watching his stomach clench.

He moaned, a throaty guttural sound that turned

her on as much as his hand sliding up her thigh. He got to the juncture and pushed her legs apart. Not that it required much effort. She wanted him inside so badly she shook with the need.

When he put his finger inside her, she arched off the bed and clutched at his shoulder. He moved so that he could watch what he was doing; spreading her nether lips and finding that one tiny nub had her ready to explode. It took seconds for her to cry out as the spasms blinded her, rocked her to the edge of oblivion. She wanted him to stop. She wanted it to last forever.

She squeezed her thighs together and he finally withdrew, slowly, reluctantly, his breaths coming raggedly on her breasts. Her eyes seemed as if they were glued shut. Her mouth wouldn't work. But she wanted more. She wanted him inside.

His muttered oath brought her around and she opened her eyes. He'd sat back and was looking around the room.

"One minute," he said, got off the bed and went to the chair with their clothes. He found his shorts, and when he fished something out of the pocket, she finally got it.

He started tearing the foil packet open on his way back to bed. She lay perfectly still, waiting, staring at the size of his erection, and gritting her teeth with anticipation. As soon as he sat at the edge of the bed, she was on the move, crawling to him, surprising him with a nip on his rear end.

"Oh." He turned around, grinning. "You wanna play rough, huh?"

She smiled coyly, and then took another nip.

"Okay." He finished sheathing himself and then lunged for her.

Laughing, she tried halfheartedly to get away. He caught her ankle and held her until he crawled on top of her, imprisoning her hip between his muscled thighs and planting his hands on either side of her head while he gazed down at her.

He smiled. "You surprise me."

"Not more surprised than me, I bet."

The corners of his eyes crinkled and he came down for a kiss, a surprisingly sweet one. He replayed the kiss on her chin, and then on her collarbone. Without warning, he slid inside of her.

Gasping, Dakota tensed at the initial impact. She relaxed, fisted the sheets and arched her back to take him in deeper. He readily accommodated her plunging so far she thought she couldn't take any more. He didn't stop, and she wouldn't have let him. Again and again he pulled out then thrust in until she was trembling from head to toe.

"Dakota," he whispered. "Now, Dakota." He threw back his head and the anguished look on his face with his final thrust gave way to a primal cry.

Anyone in the next suite could have heard it. She didn't care. An exhilarating feeling completely consumed her mind and body. Fueled her greed. She knew she'd want more. Much more. She already did.

Tony lowered himself and covered her body with his. He still suffered aftershocks, making his arms vibrate with a slight tremble. She understood completely.

"Oh, man." He looked at her, his breathing a series of short rasps. "Wow."

"Yeah." She tried to catch her own breath and moistened her parched lips.

He took it as an invitation and kissed her hard and deep before coming up for more air, and then flopping over onto his back. It took little urging on his part for her to crawl up beside him and lay her cheek on his chest.

It took only a minute longer for them to fall asleep.

"HEY." Tony touched Dakota's soft cheek and then pushed back the hair from her face.

She slowly opened her sleepy eyes. "What time is it?"

"You're on vacation. What do you care?"

"True." She smiled slowly, and then covered a yawn. "Just habit, I guess."

Still naked, they hadn't moved. She'd lain peacefully on his chest for hours. He knew the time. He'd been guilty of looking at the nightstand clock as soon as he'd awoken. Mostly out of curiosity because it was already dark outside.

She made a sleepy sound and rolled her shoulder back. "How long have you been awake?"

"A couple of hours."

She brought her head up, looking fully awake suddenly. "No."

"Yep."

"What have you been doing?"

"Watching you sleep."

She smoothed back her hair and ran her tongue over her teeth. "Tell me you're kidding."

"Why?" He urged her chin up. "You look beautiful. You always do."

Her skeptical look turned into a mischievous smile. "You, too."

"Ah, here we go." He knew she was trying to annoy him and he shouldn't react. Hell, he needed to go to the bathroom anyway.

She stopped him when he started to get up. "Okay, my timing might have been ill-intentioned, but I'm serious. Guys at my club seem to spend hours there and they don't look nearly as good as you."

He scoffed, embarrassed. "Too much sitting behind desks. All they need to do is get off their asses and do some manual work once in a while. Present company excluded." Nothing wrong with her ass, round and firm, and her breasts, crowned with those ripe pink nipples... He had to look away.

"You don't use weights?" she asked, cupping a hand over his bicep, almost reverently following the curve of the muscle.

His ego shot up a notch. "I have a couple of dumbbells at home, mostly to help me loosen up. That's it."

She smiled at him. "We're supposed to order room service for dinner."

"Hungry?"

She reached for his cock. "Not for anything on the menu."

10

THE MIX OF WHITE CLOUDS and darker brooding ones created an awesome sunset. Salmons and pinks streamed through the twilight sky and shadowed the grayish blue water below. The moon had already started to rise, tempting Dakota to run downstairs to the gift shop and buy a disposable camera.

But she was too lazy, the view from their balcony too spectacular and Tony was within arm's length of her. She looked over at him stretched out on the lounge chair just inches from her own.

"Can you believe we go home tomorrow morning?" she asked, reaching over to snag his beer.

With amusement, he watched her take a sip and then put the bottle back on his armrest. "Would you like me to get you one?"

"No, thanks. I'll just share yours."

"By all means, be my guest."

She turned and grinned at him. "I wish we could stay longer."

"Why don't we?"

"You know I can't. I have a court date on Friday and hours of preparation. I still can't believe I agreed to change our flight tonight until tomorrow morning."

He caught her hand and kissed her palm. "Aren't you glad we did?"

She nodded and sighed. "This has been the best weekend of my entire life."

"The best weekend, or the best sex?"

"Both." She gave him a mock glare. "You turkey."

He squeezed her hand. "Me, too."

"Really?"

He studied her for a moment and then frowned. "You couldn't tell?"

She withdrew her hand from his. "I don't know what your social life is like. Or how many women you're seeing. And it's certainly none of my business." She sighed. "And frankly I'm not as experienced as I should be." She pinched the bridge of her nose and tapped her head back against the lounge chair a couple of times. "I can't believe I just admitted that to you. But I'm sure you could tell."

"No more beer for you."

She shot him a puzzled look.

"No, I could *not* tell, because you were terrific. And I know because I'm probably too experienced. Not recently. In my youth." He made a face. "I don't date much now."

"Oh."

"One more thing. How experienced is one supposed to be? Is there a rule I missed?"

"I only meant that, in this day and age, a woman, like myself, who's been to college and law school and out in the workforce, well, one might expect that she's dated more than I have."

He hesitated, and she truly hoped he'd drop the subject, but that wasn't likely. He looked too curious. "Why haven't you?"

Her fault. She'd said too much. How could she possibly have become so comfortable and familiar with him? Certainly not because they'd made love at least seven times in two days. Talked about everything from terrorism to housebreaking puppies. That is, when they weren't having long, leisurely sex.

Sighing, she folded her arms across her chest. "Remember how I told you about my short rebellion in college and then finding out my mother had been right?"

He nodded, the curiosity in his eyes replaced with earnest concern.

"Well, it wasn't pretty." Most of the orange and pink in the sky had vanished because of cloud cover. The forecast for the island tomorrow was rain. A reminder that the fairy tale was over. "I'd gone with some friends to a frat party one night during my sophomore year. I knew most of the guys there. I loosely considered them friends. At the end of the night and two kegs later, two of them tried to assault me."

"Ah, Dakota."

Even in the dim light she could see the pain and rage in his face. She touched his arm. "I wasn't raped. I hadn't drunk much but they had, and I messed one of them up pretty badly."

His brows went up. "You did?"

She shrugged. "Dallas and I both had taken a lot of self-defense classes. Plus, I've always liked to kickbox for exercise."

"Damn. Nice of Dallas to have warned me." He took her hand again. "What happened?"

"I reported them. At first. But then, the dean convinced me to drop the charges. One of the jerks was a key player on the football team so they didn't want the publicity. I didn't either because I didn't want my parents to find out."

"Did they?"

"Oh, God, no. That's all I would have needed."

"You were the victim."

"Yeah, I was." She'd thought the bitterness was gone, but it coated her tongue and burned like acid in her stomach. "Remember that I was only nineteen, humiliated and scared to death my parents would find out. The two guys got slaps on the wrists and I just slunk away. That same day, all my new clothes went right into the trash."

"That wasn't that long ago. I didn't think that kind of stuff still happened to women."

"Hey, when it comes to protecting their star athletes, don't underestimate any schools' ethics." She took another sip of his beer, relieved that she was starting to feel better. "But you know what, that day, I knew without a single doubt that I wanted to study law. I wanted to be an attorney. The best one I could possibly be."

"And make sure that kind of thing didn't happen

to other women." He cupped the back of her neck and massaged the knot of tension.

She closed her eyes and let her head drop forward. "You got it."

"I thought the plan had always been for you to follow in your brother's and father's footsteps."

"The assumption was always there. Don't you dare stop," she said, when he started to remove his hand from her nape.

He continued the massage. "No, ma'am, wouldn't think of it."

"Anyway, I was a good girl and went along with what my parents wanted. I thought practicing law would be cool. But after that ordeal, it became my mission."

"I have a question."

"The answer's yes."

"Hey, I'm good but not a superhero. I have to have some time to recoup."

Laughing, she ducked away from his hand. "Okay, I'll admit it. I'm a little out of commission myself. So you're off the hook."

"Hey, let's not get crazy. I didn't mean no sex. I only meant we'll have to wait an hour."

"An hour, huh? I think I may need a couple." That was an understatement. She ached in lots of places. Really, really embarrassing places. But since tonight was their last night...

The thought stabbed at her heart. She'd miss him like crazy. No question there. But it wouldn't be practical to make plans once they returned to the city. She couldn't imagine the mountain of work that awaited her.

Worse, she couldn't imagine not seeing Tony.

Oh, God, she was in trouble.

She promptly chased all such thoughts from her mind. They were totally unacceptable. Impossible. Not wanted.

"Did you hear me?" he asked.

"What?"

"I was just saying, now don't get defensive, but aren't you letting those assholes win by caving in and dressing the way they think a woman should dress?"

"Valid point. But it's not worth the hassle. It's easier to wear a suit all the time."

"What about during off hours? Or like, while we're here. Doesn't that defeat the—"

"I admit it. I'm a coward, okay?"

He exhaled sharply. "I'm sorry. None of my business."

She didn't say anything. Better silence than to point out he was right. It was none of his business. Anyway, he didn't understand the discomfort of being hit on by married men, clients, bosses, older acquaintances of her father, for goodness' sake. Dressing conservatively and professionally made life much easier.

"Okay, next subject." He adjusted his lounge chair so that he sat upright. "Are you telling Dallas about us?"

Her heart sank. "What about us?"

"You know she's gonna ask about what happened this weekend. If you want we can tell her we didn't stay. She's not getting a bill from the hotel so she won't know the difference."

Dakota relaxed when she understood he wasn't talking about any future commitment between them. "What do you think?"

"She's your sister."

Was this a test? With the increasing darkness, she couldn't see his face very well. But she had the feeling this was more than a casual question. "We'll tell her the truth."

He faked a cough. "Like in the real truth?"

She chuckled. "How many kinds are there? We'll tell her we stayed and had a great time. I doubt she'll ask anything more personal than that."

"Okay."

"If she does…" Dakota paused. How much did she want Dallas to know? "I don't care, do you?"

A flash of white teeth and then, "Nope."

She stretched lazily. "How long did you say it would take you to recover?"

"As long as it takes you to get off your pretty butt." Tony got to his feet and pulled her up.

They'd left the air conditioner off and the sliding door open to enjoy the warm balmy breeze. Hadn't had the forethought to put on a light, though. So they stumbled into the parlor, Tony finding a lamp and switching it on.

Dakota took his hand and started to lead him to the bedroom, but he wouldn't budge. When she turned to look at him he smiled, took her face in his hands and kissed her. The kiss was so different from the others, so incredibly tender, she ached from the reminder that this would all be over soon.

Once she'd returned to her office everything would be fine. Work rarely allowed her time to think about anything else. Tonight, she'd enjoy every minute with Tony, enjoy every touch, every kiss. The endearments he used made her feel special inside.

"Shouldn't we close the drapes?" she asked once he'd moved to her ear, nibbling the fleshy lobe.

"This is the top floor. No one can see in." He reached for the hem of her tank top and drew it over her head.

She wore no bra and stood there baring herself to him, feeling not a shred of self-consciousness. How could she? Not with Tony. God, how could she be so comfortable and familiar with him in just three days? How many times had she tried to analyze the phenomenon in her head? It seemed impossible. But it wasn't.

"What are you thinking about that's making you look sad?" he whispered, cupping the weight of her breasts and kissing her lightly on the nose.

"Just wondering why you still have your shirt on." She grabbed hold of the black T-shirt and yanked it off. It ended up on the sofa with her tank top.

His expression told her he didn't believe her, but he didn't challenge her either. Instead he drew her close, her breasts pressed against his strong chest, her cheek flush with the quickening pulse at his neck.

He ran his palms down her back and rested them at the swell of her backside, just as he'd done a hundred times this weekend. Again heartwarming familiarity engulfed her. Scared her, too.

It wouldn't be easy parting tomorrow. The next couple of days would probably be lonely once she was back in her small apartment. Nevertheless, that's the way it had to be.

FIGURES THEY'D RETURN to a dreary gray day. Rain was forecast and there was a crispness to the autumn air that smelled of early snow flurries.

Neither of them had a coat, and when Tony tried to slide an arm around Dakota to warm her, she stiffened. He got the message and backed off.

"Damn, we wasted the entire plane ride," he said, yawning, as he slid in next to her in the backseat of the cab.

"What did you expect? We slept for only two hours last night."

"Was that just last night?"

She chuckled. "I know what you mean. Seems like a blur now, doesn't it?"

"Not exactly." He put an arm around the back of her seat and this time when she stiffened, he didn't give in. No one else was around. It was just the two of them, so tough. He pulled her against him. "I recall some extremely memorable moments."

She shivered, from a memory or the cold, he didn't care because she snuggled closer and that's all that counted. "Don't go there," she whispered, her breath warming his ear.

"Why not?"

"Because."

"I see."

She laughed softly, giving him a nudge with her shoulder before snuggling against him, her hand on his chest. "I hate to say it but I could probably fall asleep again."

"Go ahead." He stroked her hair. So soft. Just like the rest of her. "In this traffic, we have at least an hour before we get to Manhattan."

"What about you? Where do you live?"

"Manhattan."

"Have you always lived there?"

He shook his head. "I moved from Queens about a month ago."

"Oh."

He waited for her to say something more. He could have sworn she'd been about to ask where in Manhattan he lived. Instead she sat up and turned to look out the opposite window, putting some distance between them.

They'd come to a complete stop because of bumper-to-bumper traffic. Morning rush hour had already passed, but around here it didn't matter. She groaned. "I'm going to be so late."

"For what?"

"Work."

"You're going in today?"

She looked at him in surprise. "Sure I am. I'll probably be there until midnight trying to catch up."

"I thought maybe we'd grab a late breakfast."

"Can't."

"Early lunch?"

She smiled.

"You have to eat."

"I have granola bars in my desk drawer."

Tony looked out the other window. He'd known everything would change once they got back to the city. So why was he getting ticked off? One day at a time. His words, and this was a new day. Other choices to be made. He may not like hers, but that was too bad.

Shit.

Silence settled for a while and then she asked, "Aren't you working today?"

"Maybe tomorrow."

"Maybe?" She snorted. "Your boss may have something to say about that."

He smiled. "I doubt it."

Silence lapsed again as they both looked out their respective windows. The truth was, he had a lot of work to do, too. His new house needed some major renovations. The wood floors had been damaged from a major dishwasher leak, and the first floor walls were an ugly mint green. Even the antiquated bathrooms had to be gutted and totally redone. The stairs could wait for now but down the road they'd also need work. Not that he was complaining. Hell, no, not for the price he'd gotten the brownstone. Even though he was his own boss, he couldn't make a living by not turning over the brownstone quickly and then scooping up the next good deal. Especially in the current real estate market.

This time he broke the silence first. "Where does your boss think you've been?"

"My brother's one of the partners. Dallas handled it with him."

"What'd she tell him?"

"Something about me taking a day off to do her a favor. Believe me, Cody won't pry. He's probably too busy having his secretary pile stacks on my desk. All he'll care about is how much I can get done yesterday."

Tony shook his head. He didn't know how she could live like that. How anyone could? Deadlines on top of deadlines and everything a big rush. Allowing life to take a backseat. But it was her choice.

The rest of the ride into the city saw them alternating between yawning and chatting about everything from the Yankees to the local news overheard on the radio station playing inside the taxi.

They passed a limo on Columbus Circle, and Tony said, "Hey, that's right! How come we had to take a cab home. Where was the limo?"

"We'll have to give Dallas a hard time about that." She reared her head back, a teasing smile on her lips. "I didn't figure you for the limo type."

He snorted. "Are you kidding? Free beer, champagne, you name it."

"Yeah, and where's Otis when you need him?" She sighed, reaching for her purse when she noticed they were approaching her street.

"Hey, I have an idea. We can do this again next weekend. Same hotel. Same suite. What do you say?"

She laughed.

"I'm serious." He covered her hand when the cab

stopped. "Say the word and I'll take care of every-thing."

A small frown puckered her brows and her lips parted but she didn't say anything.

"The meter's ticking," the cab driver said over his shoulder. "Somebody getting out here?"

"Just hold on a moment," she told him sternly, and Tony smiled at her lawyerly tone. She turned back to him with regret in her eyes.

He shrugged. "It was just a thought."

"A nice one. But it won't work. I really am going to be swamped."

"I know. Hey, I should've done this already." He patted his breast pocket. The only thing in there was the napkin he'd saved from the plane. "Do you have a pen?"

She dug one out of her purse.

After scribbling his cell number, he handed it to her. "I don't have a landline, just this."

She studied the napkin for a long time, her other hand already on the door handle. Bad sign. Obviously she didn't know what to say, like, here's my number.

He swallowed his disappointment, forced a smile and kissed her on the cheek. "Don't work too hard."

"Oh, I will." She smiled sadly and opened the door. "Bye, Tony."

He nodded. That probably said it all.

11

"EXCUSE ME," Sara said as she knocked at Dakota's open door. "Would you like me to bring you back something for lunch?"

Dakota glanced at her watch. Already one o'clock. "Where are you going?"

Sara grinned, her big blue eyes sparkling. "I have a hankerin' for some of that greasy corner pizza, but I'll get you anything you like."

"Aren't you tired of that yet?"

"No, ma'am, I'm fixin' on trying the pepperoni this week." The new temp had a wide smile and fresh look about her that suited her cute southern drawl.

Dakota grabbed her purse from the bottom drawer of her desk. "There's a deli next door to the pizza place with ready-made salads. If they still have a Greek salad I'll take that, otherwise the chef salad."

"No pizza, huh?"

Dakota got up to give her some money and Sara walked in to meet her halfway. "I've lived near or in the city all my life and I've had my share, thank you."

"I suppose I'll get tired of it sometime, but I've only been here a month."

"Where from?"

"Georgia."

Cody entered the office and cleared his throat. Sara glanced over her shoulder at him, and then turned back to Dakota and made a wry face. "Be right back with your salad," she said, then as she passed Cody, her drawl exaggerated, she said, "Afternoon, Mr. Shea."

He didn't respond. At least not to Sara. He exhaled loudly and shook his head with that arrogant look Dakota disliked. "What's wrong?"

"You have to ask?" He laid a folder in the middle of her desk, on top of some briefs she'd been reviewing.

"If you're referring to Sara, I'm missing your point." She rounded the desk, sat in her chair, and made a show of moving the folder to her in-box.

He lifted one condescending brow and then, to her dismay, made himself comfortable in her guest chair. "She's not right for this office."

"Sara? You're insane. The clients love her."

"She doesn't dress particularly well, nor does she—"

"Excuse me, but Sara's a temporary employee. The firm doesn't pay them all that well." Dakota leaned back in her chair, took in his two-hundred-dollar Armani tie and the custom-made Egyptian cotton shirt. "When did you get to be such a snob?"

He stared at her for a moment, concern in his eyes. "You've been prickly *all week.* Ever since your little secret errand for Dallas. I hope she hasn't gotten you into some kind of trouble."

"Please." She sighed. "Of course not." He was right about her being prickly. He may even be right about her being in trouble. She couldn't stop thinking about Tony.

Images of him popped into her mind all the time. At work, while riding in a cab, she'd even found herself daydreaming about him in court yesterday, which was totally inexcusable. Especially when her client paid three hundred dollars an hour for her attention.

But mostly she thought about him at night when she was trying to sleep. That's when her mind proved the most susceptible. Occasionally she swore she could even feel his strong arms around her, feel his warm breath on her cheek. The sensation was both wonderful and terrifying.

"Dakota, I don't know what's wrong with you but I sure hope you pull yourself together."

She looked blankly at her brother. "Why would you say that?"

"Fine," he said wearily and stood.

"I haven't been sleeping well," she said, when she realized he genuinely did seem concerned, and then gave him a rueful smile. "Probably hormonal." That wasn't a lie.

He smiled back. "Getting old, kiddo."

"I wouldn't be throwing stones."

"Tell me about it. I found my first gray hair last week."

"Oh, you'll love looking distinguished."

Cody shot her a wary grin. "Janice and I are going to the theatre next Saturday. We have an extra ticket."

"Janice? What happened to what's her name?"

"Don't want to talk about it." He glanced down at his gray suit slacks and brushed at them. She didn't see anything but if there was a single speck of lint, Cody would find it.

"Okay. Thanks for the ticket offer but I'll have to pass."

He nodded and headed for the door where he paused. "That folder I left—there are a couple of police reports in there pertaining to the Draper case."

She swallowed, her mouth suddenly dry. "Thanks."

He left, and she sat there numb and drained. How could she have forgotten about the Draper case? She still had time, even though it meant working later than usual. What troubled her was that she'd been capable of forgetting.

The problem went back to Tony. He consumed her thoughts too often. The six days since she'd seen him had been dull. And she'd become inordinately restless. Her concentration level was probably a step above that of a puppy going from one toy to the next at lightning speed.

Suddenly paranoid, she quickly flipped through her calendar to make sure there were no other surprises coming her way. Fortunately there were none. She leaned her head back against her black leather chair and applied pressure to her temples, hoping to prevent the headache that threatened.

Tony's cell phone number was still in her purse. She should call him. Just see what he was up to. She didn't have to actually see him. But would hearing his voice be enough? Or would it whet her appetite and make her more miserable? She'd only been asking herself the same questions again and again. It was no wonder she couldn't focus. But then of course, if she did call…

God, she couldn't stand being this indecisive.

She took a deep breath and reached into the drawer for her purse. She had no choice. She had to call him. If only in self-defense.

"SON OF A BITCH!" Dropping the hammer on the workbench, Tony vigorously shook out his hand, hoping the thumb he'd just creamed would quit throbbing.

Yesterday it had been the saw he let slip. Twice in two days he'd been distracted and ended up hurting himself. He was always so careful. He'd had a perfect record, both while working for Capshaw Construction and now himself, until this week.

Damn that Dakota. Why hadn't she called? He knew she was busy with work. But would one quick phone call kill her? Probably lost his number by now. Or had thrown it away.

He went to the refrigerator and got some ice from the door dispenser. If he didn't ice down his thumb and curb the swelling, he was gonna have a hell of a time finishing this job.

He could call her if he wanted. Even though she hadn't given him her home number he knew the firm's name where she worked. But he wasn't gonna call. No way. Making the first move was hers. Hadn't she gotten all weirded out about how things would go when they got back to the city? One day at a time, he'd told her. And just for today, no way in hell he was gonna call.

Good. He'd made up his mind. He didn't have to think about it anymore. He looked at the clock. Five-fifteen. He wasn't going to get any more work done today, not with his thumb feeling as if someone had lit a match to it.

Yawning, he stretched out his aching back. He'd been putting in too many long hours. Getting to be as bad as Dakota. Her again. Sneaking her way into his brain. He had a stiff back. Nothing to do with her. Too many long hours tearing apart the bathroom.

Sleep hadn't come easy since they'd gotten back a week ago. Sometimes he lay awake all night thinking about her smile, about the weight of her breasts on his belly and chest as she crawled up his body to kiss him. To taunt him. To make him insane. He'd picture her that last evening they were on the island, lounging on the balcony at sunset, her eyes closed, her lips curved in the barest of smiles, the look of sheer contentment on her face.

That was the problem with working alone every day. Too much time to think. At least when he'd worked for Capshaw there were distractions. Joking with the guys, lunch with Dallas every day until she'd quit last year. He'd left shortly after that when his hobby of buying and refurbishing brownstones not only became more fun and challenging, but lucrative enough that he didn't need company benefits.

The sloppy wrap he'd made for his thumb slipped.

He checked the injury and decided a few more minutes of icing would help. He got to the refrigerator but before he remade the ice pack he looked in the fridge for a beer. None. What did he expect? He hadn't been shopping since he'd gotten back. Yeah, Dakota had been right. Where was Otis when Tony needed him?

Tony muttered a curse.

He backed away from the refrigerator as if it had bitten him. That wasn't the only time she'd mentioned Otis. Tony couldn't recall the time or details, but no way should she have remembered the guy. Not his name, not his spiel about keeping the fridge stocked. Otis had only been in the suite that one time—when Dakota was half-asleep and totally wasted.

So what the hell?

Dumbfounded at the sudden realization, he sat on one of the bar stools he'd had delivered yesterday. He rested his injured hand on the new brown-and-tan granite countertop he'd recently put in.

She hadn't been drunk that night. She'd known what was happening all along.

What a damn fool he was. Baffled, he replayed some of the events the night of the wedding. She'd had a few, he knew that, but why pretend she was drunk?

He stared out the window at his courtyard garden, withered and bare from the first frost they'd had last night. He just didn't get it. He didn't know if he should be angry because she'd used the pretense to shun responsibility if they were found out, or be flattered and glad that she'd gone to the extreme in order to have those few days with him.

Just when he thought he was beginning to understand her, she turned out to be a puzzle. Not that it mattered. She hadn't called. Probably wouldn't. And he wasn't sure he would either…if he could help it.

He got up and went in search of some tomato juice he thought he'd spotted earlier, when his cell phone rang. Normally he kept it clipped to his belt, but he'd put it down somewhere. He frantically looked around, locating the cell by the fourth ring.

As soon as he flipped it open, a second before he answered, he saw the unfamiliar local number and knew it was Dakota.

"Tony?"

"Hey."

"Busy?"

"Not for you." Amazing how any annoyance he'd felt just minutes ago dissolved at the sound of her voice.

She sighed. "I'm looking out of my office window at some really dark clouds. Looks like it might snow."

"I heard it would rain."

"I'm not sure which is worse."

Tony rubbed the back of his neck. "How come we're talking about the weather?"

She hesitated. "I don't know."

He knew, because he felt the awkwardness, too. No reason for it to be there. Not after everything they'd shared. But there it was. "Well, how ya doing? Working hard?"

"My eyes are crossed and I have an in-box stacked to the ceiling, but other than that everything is great."

"Sounds like you need a little R & R." Man, did he have the perfect thing in mind.

"I'll be lucky to have a whole weekend to myself from now until next summer."

"I hope you're exaggerating, Dakota."

"Not by much."

"That sucks."

She laughed. "That's an understatement. But it's not all bad. At least it's interesting work. I'm working as cocounsel on a big high-profile case."

"How big?"

"Really big. Huge."

"Would I recognize the name of your client?"

"Hmm, most likely."

"Can you tell me who?"

"Not really."

"Okay, then who's your cocounsel?"

"My brother. Why?"

No surprise there. "Just curious." Three years out of law school and already being pushed into a high-profile case. Shoved right into the limelight by Cody. At least the Sheas looked out for their own.

"I don't want to talk about work. I just wanted to see how you were doing."

Tony shook his head. It looked like he had to make the next move. "What are you doing tomorrow night? You like Italian food?"

"I've got to work, Tony."

"My grandmother taught me how to make a mean lasagna."

"Wow, a man who can cook."

"Don't get excited. I can make only five things and lasagna's the best of the bunch."

"Anything sounds better than the peanut butter and jelly sandwiches I've been eating."

"So we're on?"

"What time?"

"Your call."

"Eight-thirty too late?"

"Any time that's good for you. The lasagna can keep."

"Wait, let me find my pen. I've got to get your address."

He paced the kitchen and living room, checking out the mess he'd have to tackle before tomorrow night. His housekeeper wouldn't be back until next week. Maybe he could bribe her to come tomorrow for just a couple of hours.

"Okay, I'm ready."

He gave her the address, it turned out they lived only ten blocks apart. They hung up after that. Dakota was anxious to get her work done, and he was anxious to find his grandmother's lasagna recipe. He had no idea what the hell he'd done with it. He hadn't even finished unpacking yet. There was never any rush because he hadn't accumulated too much stuff since he moved every year or so.

Before each place was finished, he bought another one to renovate. They always sold quickly then and for more money than he'd ever pay for one. Rich people sure liked their conveniences. They wanted to be able to move in, not have to do so much as change the carpet.

He started gathering up his tools, cringing at the amount of dust he'd created changing out the dining room floor. That was the only reason he had a woman come in to clean once a week. He liked to make the mess, not clean it. But for tomorrow night he would. The kitchen was already finished and fortunately the living room didn't need that much work. He'd spruce up the downstairs bathroom and the rest of the house would have to be off-limits.

His thumb started to throb again and he went to look for his ice pack. He still couldn't believe she'd called, or that she was coming over tomorrow. Why the sudden change of heart, he wondered. Did she miss him? Or was meeting him in private kind of like being on the island. It didn't count.

DAKOTA SHUDDERED. What had she been thinking calling Tony? She didn't have time to see him. She had more work than she could handle and now she'd probably given him the wrong message and...

"Do you need anything before I leave?"

At the sound of Sara's voice, Dakota started.

"Sorry, I didn't mean to scare you," Sara said, standing in the doorway.

"I didn't know you were still here. You should've gone home already."

"It's okay. I had a few things to finish up and I'm in no hurry." Sara shrugged. "Besides, I've only been in the city a month. I don't have any friends here yet."

"Manhattan's a big change from Georgia. Are you sorry you came?"

"Oh, no. I love it here. So much to see and do."

Dakota smiled. "That's why you're working late?"

Sara laughed, flashing a cute dimple. "When I meet some people, I'll start getting out more."

Dakota nodded, a little sad for Sara. Meeting people in the city, nice people anyway, wasn't so easy.

"May I ask you a question?"

"Sure."

Sara moved in closer and lowered her voice. "Is Cody, um, I mean, Mr. Shea married?"

"Uh, no."

"Dating anyone?"

"No one seriously that I know of." Oh, God, she should lie. Tell the poor girl he's engaged. But she'd find out otherwise.

"Good."

"He's not married for a good reason." She motioned for Sara to come closer. This woman would be crushed if she went after Cody. He liked his women much more sophisticated, and with a note-worthy surname. "He's my brother and I love him, but he's high maintenance, and tends to be a bit arrogant as I'm sure you've noticed."

"Oh, yes." Sara grinned, as if she thought that flaw was cute, her blue eyes sparkling with the thrill of the hunt. "I know."

"Okay." Dakota sat back. The woman was on her own. "Just thought I'd give you a friendly warning."

"Thanks." Sara smiled and took a couple of steps back, then tucked her hair behind her ear. Dakota couldn't help but notice the woman's watch. It looked like a Rolex, but had to be a knockoff. Much too pricey for a temp's salary.

"Need anything before I leave?" Sara asked again.

"No, thank you. Go home. Salvage the evening." Dakota acknowledged her wave with a nod, and then stared at the empty doorway. Sara seemed like a nice woman, but maybe she was the type who chased after rich guys. Cody wasn't rich, but for someone like that he'd be worth the catch.

But that was *his* problem. Dakota had enough of her own. Tomorrow night she'd see Tony again. The thought both excited her and scared her to death. Her gaze was drawn to her laptop sitting on the credenza.

To her shame, she hadn't checked in with the girls at Eve's Apple since she'd been back. They were all great about sharing accounts of their dates. Not that she would be specific, but she'd at least let them know she'd gone for it.

She grabbed the laptop and brought it to her desk, placing it on top of the mess of papers she should've been working on. Instead, she flipped it open, powered up and then briefly checked her personal e-mail account. Nothing important. Nothing that couldn't wait, anyway. She switched to Create Mail and started to type.

To: The Gang at Eve's Apple
From: LegallyNuts@EvesApple.com
Subject: Mission accomplished
Hi, Everyone,
Just checking in to tell you I did it. Bit the bullet.
Had a fabulous weekend at a fabulous resort with
the most fabulous guy! All of you who told me to
go for it, you were absolutely right. Thank you.
Thank you. Thank you. It was exactly what I
needed. I'm only sorry the weekend's over. It went
way too fast. And reality just isn't quite as fun. :)

But I'm back to work, and God knows I have
enough to keep me busy. Won't have time to miss
him or the great sex, or anything else. That's the
good news. Bad news is…okay…I'll admit it. I
miss him!!!

But I'm okay. Really. No worries. Hope all is
well with the rest of you.
Your sister in arms,
D

12

DAKOTA PAID THE CABBIE and climbed out in front of
the address Tony had given her. The number she'd
written down belonged to a three-story brownstone.
Like her own apartment, the brownstone had probably been converted into three flats and rented out
separately. She searched for a directory or sign indicating which flat was Tony's, but there was only one
address etched into the eye-level bronze plaque
beside the beautiful beveled glass door, circa early
nineteen hundreds, if she weren't mistaken.

She pressed the buzzer and Tony answered the
door. He wore faded jeans and a long-sleeved navy
shirt that was too loose to give her a good view of
that great chest she'd missed all week.

"Hey, good. You're early." He stepped aside,
letting her in.

"I guess I should have called to warn you."

"Nah, the lasagna's been ready since seven-thirty,
and me…" He winked. "I've been ready for a week."

She smiled, amazed at the warmth and contentment she felt simply being in the same room with
him. He led her into the foyer, from which she could

see the living room where a cozy fire was blazing in the fireplace.

"Here, I'll take your coat."

She shrugged out of her tan cashmere with him helping. His fingers brushed the side of her neck, absurdly making her heart flutter. "I take it you have the first floor?"

"Actually, I have every floor, but this is the only one that's livable." He hung her coat in a nearby closet. "What about your blazer?"

She hesitated, and then got out of her suit jacket, leaving her in the matching gray skirt and a tailored white blouse.

He put the jacket with her coat, and then turned to her with one of those sexy grins that would have had a wiser woman running for the door. When his gaze flickered to her breasts, she realized that, even through her sensible bra and staid white blouse, her nipples were protruding.

His gaze abruptly met hers. "I have both white and red wine. Which would you like?"

"White," she murmured, backing up to give him room to pass.

The delicious smell of lasagna drifted under her nose and her stomach growled loudly. Embarrassed, she flattened a palm against the sound. It didn't help.

The noise didn't seem to faze Tony, he simply said, "I hope that sucker tastes as good as it smells."

She laughed. "You look skeptical. I thought you made a mean lasagna."

"I did. Once."

"Ah." She pressed her lips together. He looked so earnest. She didn't care how it tasted. It would be the best lasagna she ever had.

"Come in." He led her farther inside, and she followed, her gaze staying on his butt.

She hadn't seen him in jeans before. Well, once, the first time she'd met him a year ago at the job site where he and Dallas worked, but he'd been sitting down so it didn't count. But she sure was feasting on him now. She'd seen him naked so of course she knew he'd look good in jeans, but my, oh, my.

He turned and gave her an odd look, and she prayed she hadn't inadvertently said anything out loud. She cleared her throat. "This is nice." The room had high ceilings, a beige marble fireplace trimmed with ornate brass, lots of polished wood and a large Oriental rug in front of the sofa. "Really nice."

"Thanks."

"Do you own or rent?" Silly question, really. A place like this would cost a fortune.

"I bought it a couple of months ago."

"No kidding."

"A foreclosure. I got a deal." He grinned. "I wouldn't say it needs a lot of work but a tetanus shot is required to go upstairs."

She laughed. "I think I'll stay down here with the lasagna."

"You ready to eat? I just have to toss the salad and stick the garlic bread in the oven."

"For just the two of us?"

"I don't do this often, so I'm doing it right. Come in the kitchen and talk to me."

She followed him into the kitchen, again surprised by the size and quality of the granite countertops and hardwood floors. The appliances were not only new, but top-of-the-line stainless steel.

"Who the heck did you know to get a deal on this place?"

He smiled as he went around the counter to the refrigerator and got out a large glass bowl full of torn-up pieces of romaine. Except for a bottle of white wine, a bottle of ketchup and a six-pack of beer, the refrigerator looked empty.

"When I got it, the wood countertops were warped, like the floors, and the appliances were all that old avocado colored stuff from the sixties." He opened a beautiful wooden cabinet and brought out two wineglasses. "Did you say you wanted white wine?"

She nodded. "White. Thank you. Did you change the cabinets, too?"

"Oh, yeah. The old ones were ruined." He turned on the upper one of the double ovens.

The five-burner cooktop was separate, and there was a convenient butcher-block island in the center. This was a kitchen she'd kill for. If she cooked. Which she didn't.

He poured the wine with a frown, and as he passed her the glass, asked, "Are you having garlic bread?"

"I hadn't thought about it." She lied. She had. Garlic? What was he thinking?

"I don't know if I should bother heating it, because either we both eat garlic bread or neither of us do."

She tried not to smile. "Why?"

"Just in case we do a little kissing later."

"You're a little devil."

His eyes widened and his jaw dropped in mock horror. "You've been talking to my mom."

She laughed. "I figured that one out all by myself." She slowly came around the counter, her high heels clicking on the hardwood floor, and drawing his attention to her legs. "Why wait until later?"

His heated gaze slowly came up to her face. "Can't think of a single reason."

She took another step and he pulled her the rest of the way, bringing her up against him and finding her mouth with an urgency that made her dizzy. As if he couldn't get enough of her, he feverishly kissed her mouth, her chin, her neck…

"What about dinner?" she whispered.

"Mmm…" He bit her earlobe. "It tastes pretty good."

She laughed and hiccupped at the same time. "Tony, I've missed you."

"Oh, baby, not like I've missed you." He cupped her bottom and pulled her in tight. He was already hard and a vivid memory of him naked and ready for her made her whimper.

She buried her face against his neck, her palms running up his back. Feeling him through the shirt wasn't enough so she worked her way under the hem until she hit bare skin. She heard his sharp intake of breath, and then he yanked her blouse from the waist-band of her skirt.

"We should eat first," she whispered.

"Really?"

"No."

He chuckled and started unfastening her buttons. She knocked his hand away and he stopped, a startled look on his face, until she gripped his shirt again. He quickly pulled it off then went back to her buttons. She reached around and unzipped her skirt.

She didn't even know this greedy person she'd become. From the moment she'd seen him at the door she knew she wanted him stripped naked, his penis thick and hard in her hand. She wanted to taste him. Every last inch of him.

He slid her skirt down her thighs to her calves, and she stepped out of it, and then kicked off her heels. Tony moved back to unfasten his buckle.

"Nice bra," he said, the corners of his mouth twitching.

"Shut up." She'd thought about wearing one today that Dallas had bought her, but Dakota always wore a white blouse to the office and this style was appropriate.

"Very practical."

"Shut up or it stays on."

He got rid of the belt and unsnapped his jeans. "No, really, it's great. Very sexy. I'll shut up now."

"Good idea." Something caught her eye above the kitchen sink and she froze. "You don't have curtains."

"Not yet. Low on the priority list."

She looked around for her blouse, found it on the counter and pushed an arm through the sleeve.

"Now, just hold on a minute. No one can see in."

"The hell they can't. If I can see movement, then they can see in here." What on earth was wrong with her? She'd come here to have dinner. Not be dinner. She got her arm through the other sleeve but the collar was all screwed up and she turned away while she straightened it out.

"I swear to you no one can see in." He touched her arm. "I've tried myself. Just to make sure."

She got three buttons fastened and realized she'd started with the wrong hole. She muttered a most un-ladylike curse.

"Dakota?"

"What?" She didn't mean to sound so bitchy. This wasn't his fault. She was exhausted and embarrassed and…

"Dakota, look at me."

Drawing in a shaky breath, she reluctantly met his eyes.

He smiled and helped her button her blouse, correcting the ones she'd messed up. "Let's have some dinner, okay?"

No shirt, his jeans unsnapped, he stood there looking so yummy she wanted to kick herself all the way down Broadway for being a big wuss. He had to think she was a total nutcase. But being on their home turf while carrying on spooked her.

God, she felt like that one time in high school when she'd snuck out of the house to see a boy her parents had forbidden her to see. Guilt had stuck to her like wet paint for the entire two hours she was with him, and all they'd done was hold hands.

"I overreacted. I know." She thought she saw something and her gaze darted back to the window.

"No, you didn't. I'm not into being watched, either." He handed her her skirt. "Let's not allow it to ruin our evening."

She'd been about to beg out, and tell him she needed to get back to work. But he'd know better, and anyway, it wasn't fair. Not to him, and not to her, either. She'd already smiled and laughed more here, tonight, than she had all week.

Dakota stepped into her skirt, holding onto one of Tony's shoulders for support. When she went to zip it up, he silently offered to do it, reaching around her and pulling the zipper into place.

Close enough for a kiss, he seized the opportunity. She didn't refuse, didn't even glance at the window. Simply enjoyed the moment, enjoyed the warmth of his lips on hers, enjoyed the security she felt in his arms.

He kept the kiss gentle even when she tried to take it to the next level. And then he moved his mouth to her cheek for a light peck and held her tightly for a long tender moment.

Tears burned the back of her eyes. She never cried, and she sure as heck wouldn't do so now, but work pressure and exhaustion were really getting to her. And she really needed this. To be held. To not be questioned or prodded. To just be.

She inhaled deeply, composing herself, and then tilted her head back to look at Tony. "Thank you."

"You're welcome." He brushed his lips across hers. "I don't know what for, but you're always welcome."

She smiled. "Now, are you going to feed me?"

He tapped her on the backside, and then took her shoulders and turned her around. "For distracting me, you have to help with dinner. Get the plates out and toss the salad."

"I can do that." She went to the salad bowl and peered inside. He wasn't kidding. All she had to do was toss. The tomatoes and red peppers were already cut up, the black olives already sliced.

She looked up to ask him for the salad dressing, and with deep regret, saw him putting his shirt back on. Tempted as she was to ask him to leave it off, she knew that wouldn't be fair. Besides, if he humored her, she couldn't be trusted. Sighing she busied herself with looking for the dressing and found some blue cheese.

They decided to skip the garlic bread and he dished up the already warmed lasagna, while she filled salad plates. She ate so many salads for lunch at work, all she cared about was the lasagna so she made him give her an extra piece.

He took another one himself and they carried their plates into the dining room. She sat at the small oak table, which seemed completely out of place in the formal dining room, while he returned to the kitchen for their wine. The hardwood floors were in excellent shape, probably because Tony had already redone them, but the gold foil-like wallpaper was hideously gauche and old-fashioned.

"I love the wallpaper you chose," she said when he got back.

"Yeah, I was thinking about using this pattern in the rest of the house," he said with such a straight face that for an instant she thought he was serious. Then he shook his head. "You should see the stuff they had on the bathroom walls. The previous owners had lived here for sixty years. When they passed away last year, their kids mortgaged the place to the hilt for the equity because they couldn't agree on selling it, and then defaulted."

"That's sad. For all our differences, I can't imagine Dallas and Cody and I behaving that way.' She took her first bite of lasagna. "Oh, my, this is…incredible. Did you really make this?"

"Hey." He showed her the underside of his forearm. "I've got the burn marks to prove it."

She gasped playfully. The marks were faint. "Poor baby. You really did burn yourself."

He nodded, going for sympathy with a forlorn look.

"You'll live. I promise. The good news is…this lasagna is truly amazing." She took another big bite. The compliment wasn't meant to simply be nice. The man could cook.

They talked very little while they continued eating, and too late, she realized she'd eaten too much. Walking home instead of taking a cab would help that problem, but damned if her mind didn't go straight for another way to burn off some of her dinner. Surely he had to have curtains in his bedroom.

"Okay," she said, getting up with her plate and reaching for his. "The least I can do is the dishes."

He immediately got to his feet and took the plates from her. "Domestic goddess that you aren't, you probably haven't heard of one of these newfangled inventions. It's called a dishwasher."

"Wow, imagine." She grabbed their glasses and followed him to the kitchen. Her gaze went directly to the window. Nothing there, of course, but she couldn't help it. "Hey, you drank wine tonight."

"It goes with lasagna. Has to be red, though. Just ask my grandmother." He stacked the plates in the sink, and she grabbed a dish towel. "Another thing I should explain about these dishwashing contraptions, you always let the dishes soak in the sink first." He took the towel out of her hand and threw it on the counter.

"I hadn't heard that one before."

"Trust me." He took her hand and led her into the living room.

At his urging, she sat on the overstuffed leather couch and then watched him look through a rack of CDs. His shirt was untucked and to her knowledge he hadn't put his belt back on. She laid her head back, drowsy from her carb-fest, knowing she should go home, knowing she couldn't leave yet.

"You like Norah Jones?" he asked, and then turned around when she didn't answer.

"I'm trying to think. I know I've heard her before."

"She has a distinctive voice." He slid the CD into

the player. "If you've heard her before, you'll recognize her immediately."

He left on one dim lamp, and turned off the rest of the lights. Then he joined her on the couch, angling himself toward her and pulling her back against his chest.

"If you fall asleep, I'll wake you in an hour," he whispered, his chin lightly resting on top of her head, his strong arms encircling her, crossed gently over her breasts, and imprisoning her arms.

She didn't feel trapped, though. Safe and content, yes. The only scary thing was how easy it would be to forget the responsibilities and pressure of work. But she knew better. Tomorrow morning's meetings and deadlines would come and she'd better be ready.

She turned so that her cheek rested against the base of his throat, and snuggled deeper, bending her elbows so that she could curl her hands around his forearms. She wouldn't go to sleep, but it was nice listening to the bluesy voice of Norah Jones and feeling Tony's strong heartbeat, which was the last thought she remembered having.

ADMITTEDLY, Tony had had other plans for the evening. But this was good. He liked holding her and knowing that for just a little while she wasn't thinking about work. She could relax and know she was safe, and that he was right here if she needed him.

Her grip on his forearms slackened and he knew she'd drifted off. Probably not for long, but a power nap always did him a world of good. He inhaled the vanilla scent of her shampoo, laid his head back and closed his eyes. It would be easy for him to fall asleep, too. After working a twelve-hour day himself, one glass of wine and a plate of pasta was enough to do him in. But he couldn't break his promise to wake her.

He quickly stifled a yawn when his chest expanded and she stirred. He tightened his arms around her ever so slightly and she settled down, and he lay back again, enjoying the feel of her soft breasts beneath his arms.

He could hear her gentle breathing.

Or maybe it was his own.

The voice of Norah Jones lulled him into a pleasant twilight. He fought sleep. Blinked several times to keep himself awake. But his lids felt so damn heavy....

TONY WASN'T SURE what startled him. He opened his eyes. It took a second to realize he was still on the couch. Dakota was with him. And she was unzipping his jeans.

"Good morning," she whispered.

"Is it?"

"Two-fifteen."

"I'm sorry."

"Don't be." She pushed his shirt up and found his nipples.

He smiled. "Come here."

She shimmied up to him, causing unbearable friction in her wake. "Yes?" she said, her lips against his mouth.

While he kissed her, he pulled her blouse from the waistband of her skirt and then unzipped her. She helped him with the annoyingly small buttons of her blouse and he helped her pull off his jeans. Her panty hose was the biggest challenge and he wasn't sure but he might owe her a new pair. But in spite of all obstacles, within seconds they were both naked.

Thank God he'd left the old drapes up.

She ran two fingers along his cock. "Tony, do you have any—?"

He shuddered. "Yep, give me a minute." He got up even though he had condoms in his jeans pocket, but he didn't think it would be cool to just whip them out. Might give her the wrong idea.

He disappeared for a few seconds and when he got back he found her looking over his CD collection. In full light, she was perfect. Standing there, naked, in the dim glow of the lamp, she looked like an artist's rendering. From the graceful curve of her neck to the seductive curve of her backside, she was perfection. Even her sexily tousled hair looked as if it had been arranged. But he knew for sure it hadn't. Not Dakota.

She looked up and smiled. And that was perfect, too.

He couldn't wait. Not another minute.

Taking her hand, he brought her back to the couch, urging her to help sheath him. He kissed her hard and deep, and holding her hips, guided her over him. He stretched his legs out as she straddled him, lowering herself until he entered her, so slick and wet that in three thrusts the explosion started.

13

NOBODY HAD GOTTEN to the office yet. Only six-fifteen. Early even for Dakota. But she badly needed to get a jump on the day. Yesterday, after leaving Tony's place at four in the morning, she'd gotten only two hours sleep before going to the office. The whole day had gone downhill with her first cup of spilled coffee.

She'd functioned at half speed, managing to get in only six hours of work after putting in a twelve-hour day. Last night she'd crashed early when she was supposed to have been preparing an opening argument. Fortunately, she'd always been an early starter so she wasn't late with it yet.

The coffeemaker in the room next to her office made that low gurgling sound it always did when the coffee was done brewing and she went to get a cup before she unloaded her briefcase.

On the way back, her laptop caught her eye. It normally took downing half a cup of strong Colombian brew before she could function anyway, so she saw no harm in checking for responses from the Eve's Apple gang.

She got set up and relaxed in her chair as the

messages started popping up. Jeez, she'd never seen so many responses, most of them calling her an idiot judging by the subject lines. Did she really want to read those?

Curiosity got the better of her and she chose a few to read while she sipped her coffee.

To: LegallyNuts@EvesApple.com
From: Cindy@EvesApple.com
Subject: Who are you kidding?
D,
You're not okay. Reread your e-mail. Be honest with yourself. I felt so sad reading it. Are you seeing this guy again? What happened!?!
Cindy, who's on your side but doesn't get it

That one stopped her. How much had changed in just one day! Yeah, she'd seen Tony again, but what had that accomplished? She liked him even more if that were possible. But that solved nothing. In fact, she'd probably have been better off not contacting him again. To think he lived so close was sheer torture. That in a ten-minute cab ride she could be with him. Kissing him. Be in his arms. Feel the stress miraculously melt away just because he was near.

She looked to the next message, this one with a more neutral subject line.

To: LegallyNuts@EvesApple.com
From: HornyInHenderson@EvesApple.com
Subject: Hey!!!

D,
You really are nuts if you don't think we all don't want to hear more about the weekend. Details, please!!!!!!!!!!!!!

BTW listen to Cindy. She's right.
Love and kisses,
Horny

Dakota shook her head. Details they definitely weren't going to get. She was about to get offline when she recognized the moniker of a woman who'd e-mailed her the first time Dakota had posted. She couldn't resist seeing what BabyBlu had to say and promised herself this was the last one she'd waste time reading.

D,
I'm glad to see you've posted again. I've been thinking about you a lot lately. Better than thinking about how miserable I am, eh? <G> I saw Larry the other day. He was with a woman. She had on an engagement ring. Nice emerald cut, maybe three-quarters of a carat, two small baguettes on the side. Nothing like the two-carat solitaire I bought myself last month for closing a big sale. Good thing I could afford it. No one else to buy me a ring. <<sigh>> I'd trade it for a pop top ring if Larry had given it to me. God, I miss him. So, have you broken down and seen your man again? If not, do it. Don't wait until you see him walking around with some other chick.

Let us hear from you again.
Good luck!
Love,
Carson

Dakota signed off, feeling the same sadness she experienced the last time she'd read Carson's e-mail. Worse, this time, she felt the threat of panic. Could she stand seeing Tony with another woman? It would kill her. Not that she had a speck of right to feel anything but indifference. That knowledge didn't lessen the gnawing in her gut.

The irony was that it could easily happen. They lived in adjoining neighborhoods. Not often, but at times she went up to his corner market for produce or this special cheese she couldn't find anywhere else.

Then again, maybe he wouldn't stick around the Upper West Side. He might have gotten a good deal on the house, but excluding the kitchen, it still needed a lot of work and, from the look of it, he'd run out of money. Plus he had his day job. The renovation could take years.

She had to stop speculating. It did no good and she had too much work to do. If Cody asked her for the first draft of the opening argument one more time, she'd scream.

She heard the elevator ding, which meant her peace and quiet was about to end. So was her chance to get a head start on the day. She was so screwed.

TONY HAD KEPT his cell phone close for two days. No calls from Dakota. Bad enough she hadn't woken him up before she left the other night, but she hadn't given any indication if or when they'd see each other again.

He knew she was busy and under a lot of pressure. And he didn't even mind seeing her on her terms until things settled down for her at work. But she could at least call. He was tired of misplacing his tools because his mind had drifted off, wondering about her. Like his level. He looked on his workbench and then on the dining room table. Second time today he'd misplaced that same level. What the hell had he done with it now?

It wasn't on the bathroom counter, but he did find a hammer he'd been looking for an hour ago. His missing tool belt hung over the doorknob. This had to stop. At this rate, he'd still be working on the house five years from now.

Maybe she was waiting for him to call. She'd made the last move. His turn. He'd already programmed her work number into his phone. Unfortunately it wasn't a direct line and he had to go through the company operator. He waited for the woman to connect him, half expecting to get a voice mail. But Dakota answered, by briskly stating her name.

"Prove it," he said in a gravelly voice.

"Pardon me?"

"Prove you're Dakota Shea."

She hesitated and then laughed. "Let's see…I know this guy named Tony, and I could tell you something really juicy about him that only I would know."

"Okay, okay. I believe."

"I was just thinking about you," she said, her voice

lowering, and then through the phone line, he heard a door close.

Smiling, he sat down on the couch and swung his legs up, not caring about his dusty jeans or work boots. "What were you thinking about?"

"About how late you kept me up the other night and how behind I am at work because of you."

"I kept you up?" He snorted. "I remember quite a different scenario. Like waking up to one hell of a surprise."

She issued a short laugh. "Shh."

"Nobody on this end to hear me, darlin'."

"Okay, I give up. Mea culpa."

"So when are you coming over and mea culping me again?"

She made a tsking sound. "You are so bad."

"Isn't that what you like about me?"

"Probably." She sighed. "Hey, I have—"

She stopped at the same time Tony thought he heard a knock at her door. A man's voice mumbled something about a meeting, and then she was back on the line.

"Tony, I've got to go," she said, papers rustling in the background.

"No problem."

"Thanks for calling."

He didn't like that brusque tone. "How about a drink after work?"

She didn't answer. Even the papers quieted. "Just a quick one, Dakota. Wherever you want."

She sighed. "Okay, I can dash out around six but

I'll have to come back to the office later. Do you know Sargenttis?"

"I know it." A hoity-toity place near Wall Street he'd been to a couple of times. Not of his own choosing.

"Okay."

"See you there."

She hung up first. Almost before he'd finished talking. He didn't take offense. He knew she was busy and that's why he hesitated to call her at work. But she still hadn't given up her home number. Maybe tonight when they met for a drink.

Sargenttis, huh?

Yeah, he knew it. And she wanted to meet there? Interesting.

DAKOTA CHECKED HER WATCH and punched the elevator button again. She was already five minutes late and the bar was another five-minute walk away. She was out of her mind for telling Tony to meet her there. Talk about lawyer central. She didn't go for after-work drinks often, but when she did, it was always to Sargenttis because it was basically the only bar she knew, and only because all the other attorneys went there.

Including her brother. Great. Just great.

Luckily, Cody was still in a meeting. But there would be other colleagues there. And there'd be questions and curious looks and Tony would end up feeling uncomfortable.

It was her fault. She'd gotten flustered when Cody had poked his head in to remind her about the meeting. She'd been gathering the necessary paperwork for it when Tony called. And poof, just like that, everything else flew out of her mind. And in that moment of weakness, she'd suggested the popular bar.

She so wished she had Tony's cell number with her. Fine place for it to be, sitting on her nightstand. All because last night she'd been tempted to call him but had consistently talked herself out of it.

She got half a block away from Sargenttis and pulled off the clip that was holding her hair back. She fluffed the flat strands as she walked, moistening her lips and wishing she'd remembered to apply lipstick before she left the office.

A man in front of her opened the door for both of them and welcome warm air hit her face. In that instant she realized she'd forgotten her coat. She'd walked three blocks in only her suit and it had to be forty degrees.

She was losing it.

The bar was crowded, lots of expensive suits and loud talking. She couldn't actually hear anyone specifically, but she recognized two judges, neither of whom was her favorite, and several self-important attorneys who worked in her building. At a corner table, two of her office colleagues were engaged in conversation.

She didn't see Tony, even as she walked past the group of tables that bordered the ornate turn-of-the-century bar. It was hard to see who sat in the booths but more than one person occupied each one.

She finally spotted him at the end of the bar surrounded by three men and a woman, only one of whom she knew. A black leather jacket hung off the back of Tony's bar stool, and he wore a white T-shirt and jeans and laced-up work boots, clean, not as if he'd just gotten off work or anything, but he looked totally out of place in a sea of expensive tailored fabric. Obviously it didn't bother him. He seemed completely at ease and involved in a lively conversation with the others.

If only she felt that comfortable having him here among her peers. The thought shamed her, briefly, but the truth was that her career was important to her and it was more complicated than just being a good lawyer.

She approached quietly and stood off to the side, hoping to eavesdrop, hoping Bruce, the one guy she did know, wasn't being his usual pain in the ass. He was young, brash, successful and full of himself, but insecure enough that he had to make sure everyone else knew of his successes.

"So, Greta, when are you thinking of taking the plunge?" Tony asked the thirtyish blond woman who was part of the group.

"I'm thinking spring. Any thoughts?"

Tony shrugged. "Any time is good if the price is right."

"Amen." Bruce tipped his head back and drained his martini, and then signaled the bartender for another.

"Yes, but you're talking about a place that needs work. I can't manage paying rent and financing renovations and overseeing the work," Greta explained.

"Look, this is what you do—" He saw Dakota

and a warm smile curved his sexy mouth, making every one of his companions turn toward her direction. "Dakota. Hi."

She felt her cheeks flame. Thank goodness the bar was dimly lit. "Hi." She swung her gaze around to include everyone, and then nodded at Bruce.

Tony slid off his bar stool. "Here, I was saving this for you."

"Thank you."

He stood with the guys. She sat beside the blonde.

"I'm Greta." She offered her hand. "That's Derrick and Sam. We're with Simon and Lloyd."

"I work with Bruce at Webster and Sawyer." Dakota caught the amusement in Tony's eyes. It was professional courtesy to let the other person know for whom you worked.

She thought for a second. Not that it really mattered, she supposed. But when you worked for a prestigious firm it was kind of a high to see the trace of envy in people's eyes.

"May I borrow him for just a few more minutes?" Greta asked, and without waiting for a reply, turned back to Tony. "You were saying about doing a renovation?"

"This is yours," Tony said to Dakota. He'd apparently ordered her the white wine that was sitting on the bar.

She'd planned on drinking orange juice since she had to go back to work, but she smiled her thanks and took a small sip.

He winked and turned back to Greta. "This is what

you do. After you buy the place, you choose one room that you have to have right away, like the bedroom or kitchen, wherever you spend the most time. You get that done before you move in, and then do the rest slowly as you can afford it."

The bartender came with Bruce's martini and put a beer in front of Tony. Just the bottle. No glass. "This is from Mr. Wilson," he said, indicating Bruce.

"Thanks, buddy." Tony gave him a nod, and then said to Greta. "You need to find a good contractor you can trust, so that most of the work can be done while you're at the office."

"Makes sense." Greta smiled. "How about you? Would you be interested in the job?"

"No, ma'am." Chuckling, Tony shook his head. "I've got enough on my plate."

"You didn't finish telling me what to do about the bottom of my boat," Sam said, and Tony gave Dakota an apologetic look before launching into an explanation about the quality of marine paint and barnacle removal.

Dakota didn't mind. She liked listening to him. He seemed to have quite an extensive knowledge of a variety of do-it-yourself improvements. Even Bruce, who was never interested in a conversation unless it was about him or his current case, seemed absorbed by Tony.

"I'm thinking about building a summer house on some land I have on Martha's Vineyard," Bruce said. "Any ideas on how I could save a few bucks without cutting corners?"

"Yeah, don't let anyone talk you into a slab foundation. A crawl space is cheaper. And quit drinking seventeen-dollar martinis at Sargenttis."

Everyone laughed, even Bruce, who then saluted Tony with his seventeen-dollar martini.

"My ride is leaving. I have to go." Greta hurriedly laid a couple of twenties on the bar near her wineglass. "Nice talking to you, Tony." She slid off her stool and whispered to Dakota, "He's adorable. Where'd you find him?"

Dakota just smiled, and then watched Greta join an older man waiting at the door.

The men had already started a lengthy discussion about cars. Dakota took another small sip of wine and then asked the bartender for a glass of water. When she turned around again, she found Tony staring at her.

He smiled. "Everything okay?"

"Perfect."

"You want to get out of here?"

"I'm fine." In fact, the more he talked, the more she liked listening to him. His charm mixed with enthusiasm made even the most tedious discussion interesting. Even Sam mentioned that Tony should host one of those do-it-yourself television shows that had become so popular.

Bruce tried to buy Tony another beer, which he declined. "Anything this guy doesn't know?" Bruce asked, shaking his head.

"Well, while you pretty boys were going to college and partying I was actually reading books."

The guys laughed good-naturedly.

"Well, I'm outta here. Almost dinnertime." Sam signaled the bartender for his tab. "My wife is pregnant and expected me home on time."

"Been there, done that." Derrick ordered another drink.

Tony subtly turned so that he gave the other two his back. "You're quiet."

She smiled. "Like I've had a chance to say boo."

"Uh, yeah, sorry."

"I'm teasing."

"You know I'd much rather be talking to you." The way he looked at her, his eyes so intense, it was as if he'd touched her. He hadn't, not once, even though she knew he wanted to.

She appreciated his restraint, his knowing how awkward it would be for her. Glancing around, she saw that several other colleagues from her office had arrived. But not Cody, thank goodness. He generally worked too late to stop at the local bar but there was always that possibility.

But even if he did, so what?

She took another quick look around, wishing she could be that blasé.

Tony took another sip of his beer. "I seriously think we should go someplace else. Maybe get some dinner. I know this place in midtown that—"

Dakota shook her head. "I have to go back to the office."

"Tonight?"

She nodded. "That's why I suggested this place."

"Bummer."

"Yeah." She saw Bruce wander over to a secretary who worked on the floor below them. "How did you end up talking to those guys?"

"This bar," he said, knocking on the polished wood, "was constructed with pieces of wood from an old Italian vessel. I was asking the bartender what he knew about it, and they overheard."

"How did you know about the wood?"

"I don't know. I was trying to remember that myself." He frowned over his shoulder and then leaned closer. "What's with introducing yourselves along with the name of the firm you work for? Is there some kind of hierarchy with you guys that us mere mortals don't know about?"

She made a face at him. "Funny."

"No, seriously, that was kind of a trip the way you and Greta traded employer information. Is it kind of like my dad can beat up your dad?"

She rolled her eyes at him. "It's hard to explain," she said and checked her watch, eager to drop the subject. It was a little embarrassing.

"Okay," he said. "Have you heard from Dallas?"

"No, but I don't expect to until day after tomorrow. That's when she gets back."

"Ah." He took another sip of his beer.

Silence stretched and she realized he was waiting for her to say something. Only she'd been distracted by the guys from the office who'd taken a corner table. They had to have seen them.

"So what time do you think you'll get done tonight?" He leaned close enough to unsettle her, but not enough that anyone could draw a conclusion.

"I don't know. Late. Really late."

"Did I tell you I'm a night owl?" There was that sexy undermining grin again.

"I can't, Tony. I also have an early morning meeting."

"Sure. I understand." He lowered his voice. "This is hard. Not being able to touch you."

"Yeah, I know." She made a quick grab for her wineglass and took a big gulp. She couldn't give in. She really did have an early meeting tomorrow. "In fact, I have to be going."

"Already?"

"Hey, Mr. Goodwill Ambassador, I'm not the one who started a new social club."

"I'm not the one who showed up late."

"Touché." It'd turned out well, actually. Being part of a group with him was so much better for appearances. Sighing, she got off her stool. "Believe me, I'd much rather be here with you than slaving away in my office. But I don't have that choice."

"Hey, I'm glad I got to see you." He reached into his jeans pocket, the T-shirt pulling tightly across his chest, and she swallowed. Not a man in this room could fill out a T-shirt like that. "Hold up. I'll settle the check and walk you back."

"No. Stay," she said quickly. Maybe too quickly judging from his narrowed gaze. "You didn't finish your beer." Meeting him here was one thing, but she couldn't walk out with him. How would it look?

"Really. I'll call," she added, briefly touching his hand, and then resisted the urge to see if anyone had been watching.

"Okay." He smiled. "I'll talk to you later."

God, she wanted to kiss him.

She abruptly turned and walked toward the door, keeping her gaze straight ahead, acknowledging no one as she left the bar. Once she got outside, she felt this weird emptiness in the pit of her stomach and had the sudden urge to hail a taxi, go home and crawl under the covers.

Ironic really. She'd thought Tony would be a problem, but the problem turned out to be her. Right now, she didn't like herself very much.

14

TONY STOOD BACK and admired the new floor he'd just put in the guest bathroom. He'd gotten a good deal on some discontinued tile and was able to use a higher quality than he'd anticipated. His supplier was looking into another possible discontinued batch for the master bath. A few breaks like that would up his selling price.

He heard a knock at the door and pulled off his work gloves. His mother and sister had been the only visitors he'd had other than Dakota. Against all odds, he hoped like hell it was her. But it was the middle of the day and she didn't even know how to knock off work at a decent time, so he wasn't holding his breath.

Besides, two days since he'd seen her at Sargenttis, and she still hadn't called. She was busy—he got that. But one lousy phone call?

Glancing through the peephole, he saw that it was his Realtor wrapped in that mink coat she started wearing the second the temperature dipped below sixty-five, and he reluctantly opened the door.

"Finished yet?" she asked, and walked past him, heading straight for the kitchen.

"Hi, Sylvia, nice to see you, too." He shook his head and closed the door. The woman could sometimes be too pushy for his taste, but she got results and had made him a lot of money.

"Oh, my God, Tony. This granite is to die for. Where did you find it? I know you didn't get it from that skunk on Fourth." She waved a dismissive hand. "He wouldn't know quality if it bit him in the face."

"As a matter of fact, I did get it from Manny. Gave me a good deal, too."

She narrowed her gaze, her eyes so heavily made up it made her look ten years older. "I very nicely asked him to look into some discount floor covering for me to put in one of my rentals and that worm told me…" She pulled herself up straight, lifting her chin. "I'm a lady so I won't repeat what he told me."

Tony grinned. "What can I do for you, Sylvia?"

"You can finish this job. I have a buyer."

"You what?"

"Don't worry. He's not in a rush."

Tony glanced around the room. "I didn't even decide to sell this one yet."

Her dark brows drew together in outraged disbelief. "What else would you do with it?"

"I don't know." He shrugged. "Keep it maybe."

"Tony, don't be foolish."

"Owning a piece of real estate in Manhattan is foolish?"

"You know what I mean. The market is hot right now. You've made an awful lot of money, and there's a lot more to be made."

"Sylvia, the market's always hot in Manhattan. Besides, it's not all about money."

She frowned, studying him closely. "Of course it is."

He scoffed. "Says you."

"Remember when you first came to me and asked for comps on listings and you said—"

"Okay, okay, but my only goal was to eventually quit construction and support myself this way." Hell, he didn't have to explain anything to her. She made her commission. A damn good one.

"And you're doing a great job. By the way, you look tired. Aren't you sleeping?"

He checked his watch. "I really have to get back to work."

"Can you spare some time for lunch? I'm buying."

"Already ate. But thanks." He started toward the door. She got the hint and followed, and he said, "Look, I don't know what I'm going to do yet. I'll probably sell, but if I don't, I'll find another one to turn over."

"All right." She sighed, then her expression suddenly brightened. "My niece is coming to town this weekend, a real pretty girl, and—"

He opened the door. "Goodbye, Sylvia."

She drew the front of her mink coat together at the throat. "Call me," she said, before hurrying out to a waiting cab.

Tony closed the door. He really hadn't eaten and since he was at a stop he went to the kitchen to make himself a peanut butter and jelly sandwich. His cell rang twice before he was done. Both calls were from guys where he used to work wanting to go for a beer at four. He left it open, telling them that he'd probably make it, but not to send a search party out if he didn't.

He still had the old-fashioned claw-foot tub and ancient commode to move out of the master bath. Later, a couple of buddies he'd hired for extra muscle were coming to help. They always showed up when he called, but never at the requested time. Otherwise, it would be nice to see his old coworkers. It had been a while.

Not since before Dallas's wedding. Since before Dakota had started making him nuts. Shaking his head, he carried his sandwich and a bottle of water to the table. When she'd asked him to meet her at Sargenttis, he'd been pretty surprised. He knew it was a lawyer hangout. Twice he'd had lunch there with his own attorney.

Foolishly he'd hoped the ice was finally broken. That she'd acknowledge they had a developing relationship. But she hadn't been comfortable being there with him. Too subdued, and the constant wary looks around the room she tried to disguise had been disappointing. Maybe it had nothing to do with him. Or maybe the way he'd been dressed embarrassed her.

He'd thought about putting on dress slacks and a nice sweater. God knew he had enough of them, mostly Christmas presents from his mom and sister. But he'd resisted. That wasn't him. He liked the comfort of T-shirts and jeans and he wasn't about to change. Not for anyone. This was him. Take it or leave it. No matter what, she got major points for inviting him in the first place.

Half his sandwich was gone and he didn't remember tasting a single bite. He was tired of peanut butter and jelly anyway. Tonight he'd order in Chinese. Maybe Dakota would miraculously call or show up.

Damn, he shouldn't have made that crack about her and Greta bringing up which law firm they worked for. It was weird though. Kind of like their jobs were their identities. He didn't get it. But it was none of his business and he should've kept his mouth shut.

What if Dakota had overheard Sylvia today? Her claim wasn't true. He loved what he did. No way was it about the money. But man, Dakota could've had a lot of questions, a lot of cracks to make herself. Being able to afford whatever he wanted was nice. Damn nice. But that hadn't been his goal. He just wanted to be his own boss and still make a living.

Simple.

He looked at the beautiful new hardwood floor beneath his boots, and experienced a rush of satisfaction for a job well done. One of the things he liked best about his work was the immediate gratification. With his hands, he created something beautiful out of nothing. That's what life was all about. Personal satisfaction.

Money was the gravy. He inhaled deeply. Easy to say, however, because what he liked to do paid well. Would he still love it without the money?

"I'LL NEED THIS by three-thirty." Dakota handed Sara a thick folder of papers she needed copied.

"They'll be ready. I have something for you to sign, too." Sara gave her a bright smile that was quickly transferred to something behind Dakota.

She turned around. Cody was headed toward them.

She quickly signed the request she'd made for an additional temp. "Thanks. I ordered a sandwich to be delivered. This should be enough including tip." She hastily set down some money on Sara's desk, hoping to head Cody off.

He was really bugging her lately, always stopping by her office over the most minute thing, as if he were checking up on her. That really ticked her off.

He was already behind her. "Got a minute, Dakota?" he asked, his gaze straying to Sara.

"Only one."

Cody didn't seem to notice Dakota's abrupt tone. His gaze stayed on Sara. "I didn't get a hold of those tickets." he stated.

Sara sighed and shook her dark head. "Maybe next time."

"If I hear anything, I'll let you know." Cody continued to focus on the secretary.

Although he sounded slightly gruff, Dakota knew her brother better than that. She stared at him for a moment, bewildered by the way he seemed in no hurry to get down to business, instead lingering near Sara's desk. Maybe his constant dropping by had nothing to do with Dakota. Maybe he just wanted to see Sara.

Dakota silently laughed at herself. She seriously

needed more sleep if she thought for one moment...
Maybe when hell froze over.

She led the way into her office, but apparently he
was in no hurry to follow her. He showed up a minute later.

"What was that about?" Dakota asked.

He sat across the desk from her. "What? Oh,
nothing. Your temp—"

"Sara."

"Yeah, Sara. She wanted tickets for a sold-out show.
I thought I knew someone who didn't want theirs."

"Ah." Interesting that they'd talked long enough
to get on the subject in the first place.

Her amusement must have shown because he was
suddenly all business and cranky, at that. "Dakota,
frankly, I'm concerned about you," he said lowering
his voice, unsettling her.

She leaned back in her chair. "Why?"

His eyebrows rose. "You're distracted. You're
barely meeting deadlines."

"Barely being the operative word." Okay, this conversation was going to be bad. Her temper sparked
and her defenses shot up as high as they could go.

"It's not like you. Usually you're more focused."

"I am focused."

He smiled. "You know better."

"Don't give me the big-brother you-can't-fool-
me look. It'll only make me angry."

"I'm also your boss, and I need to know that
you're committed to working the Draper case."

She shook her head in utter disbelief. "You're questioning my commitment."

"This case isn't just important to this firm, it's a major stepping stone in your career."

"I'll worry about my own career, thank you." She fell silent, trying to rein in her anger and battling the acceptance that he was partially right. She wasn't as focused as she should be.

He let her have her quiet for a while and then sighing heavily said, "I hear you've been seeing Tony. Could that be the reason for your distraction?"

"Who told you that?"

"Someone mentioned you met a guy at Sargenttis. From his description, that guy Tony is the only person like that we know."

Blood surged to Dakota's face.

When she thought she could speak without biting his head off, she said, "Explain what you meant by 'only guy like that we know.'"

He briefly closed his eyes, shaking his head. "You know what I meant."

"I sincerely hope it's not what I think. I'd hate to find out you're truly that big an ignorant snob."

"You're overreacting."

"Funny, I was thinking the same about you."

"Okay, I see this is going nowhere." He got to his feet while straightening his obscenely expensive Prada tie. "We'll talk later."

"Not about this subject. As my boss, my private life is none of your business. As my brother, I love you, but it's still none of your business." She paused to take a deep shuddering breath. "And don't ever question my commitment to this case or this firm again."

He said nothing, just walked to the door. Before he left, he turned around and asked, "Have you heard from Dallas?"

Taken aback by the innocuous question, she could only stare while gathering her thoughts. "Yes, this morning. They got in late last night so we only talked for a minute."

He nodded absently, and then disappeared from her doorway.

Probably went to sweet-talk Sara, the hypocrite. Well, he had at least one redeeming quality. He cared enough to ask about Dallas.

Why was Dakota angry or even surprised? Hadn't she expected fallout from meeting Tony at Sargenttis? Maybe she had some crazy desire to be outed and that's why she'd chosen that bar?

Outed? The unexpected thought sickened her. Tony wasn't a dirty secret. He was her friend. God, she was as bad as Cody. Must be a faulty Shea gene.

She rubbed her throbbing temple. The truly horrible reality was her brother being right about the distraction part. It wasn't as if she hadn't given the case adequate attention. It simply had taken twice as long to do it. Cody was also right about this particular case. Winning could do more for her career than having been in the top five of her graduating class in law school.

The painful truth was, she didn't have time for Tony right now. Even more painful, she didn't know that she ever would.

"DALLAS?"

"Tony!"

"Is this a bad time?"

"No. I'm glad you called."

He hadn't expected to catch her and put down his chopsticks. Dinner could be zapped in the microwave later. "How was the honeymoon?"

"You have to go sometime. It was an amazing experience. No unpacking or cooking or making my bed for two whole weeks."

He chuckled. "Didn't care for the scenery, huh?"

"That was a whole other amazing. I swear at every turn in the Rhine there was another castle. We have tons of pictures. I can't wait to bore you. You and Dakota will have to come over for drinks soon."

That stopped him. Had she talked to Dakota? "Sure, count me in."

"Well, so how was *your* vacation?"

"Have you talked to Dakota?"

"This morning."

"How did she say it went?"

Dallas laughed. "I only talked to her for a few minutes. I was wiped out from traveling and she was at work, sounded busy."

That made him feel better. Dakota really was busy and not just chumping him. Then again maybe Dallas was backpedaling and didn't want to hurt his feelings by having to repeat her conversation with her sister. Not that he'd ask her to.

"So, I take it you stayed the weekend?"

"Yeah, we stayed."

"Good." Obviously Dallas wanted to ask more questions. Which made him think she really hadn't talked to Dakota after all. But to her credit, all she asked was, "Anything else going on?"

He smiled at her subtlety. "Nothing I can think of. Just wanted to make sure you were back safely."

"Safe and happy." She sighed a contented sigh. "Can you believe I'm married?"

"Yep. You guys are a good team."

She paused. "You and Dakota getting along okay?"

"We got along great," he said, deliberately using the past tense. He wasn't going to say any more. Anything more she'd have to get from Dakota.

"Call her, Tony. Trust me on this, okay?"

He didn't want to go there. "I ordered Chinese and it's getting cold." So was his bed.

"All right, you coward. Go eat."

"See ya, Dallas."

She tsk-tsked. "See ya."

He hung up, set aside the phone and stared at his cold chow mein and kung pao chicken. It wouldn't hurt to call her. The worst that could happen is that she'd tell him to go to hell.

The switchboard was probably closed, he realized when the fifth ring went unanswered. She still hadn't given him her private line and he was about to hang up when surprisingly Dakota answered.

"Hey, you playing operator?"

"She goes home at six."

"Smart lady."

"Yeah, except anyone working late ends up having to answer."

"Which is pretty much always you."

"There's still a lot of us here. Even two of the partners are working late."

"Shining examples."

She sighed. "Did you call to harass me?"

"Oh, baby, that is so not what I had in mind to do to you."

She laughed. "Hold on. Let me get back to my office."

He heard a click and then a few seconds later she was on the line again.

"I was passing my assistant's desk when the main line rang so I grabbed it out there," she said. "We kind of take turns but it's usually pretty quiet after six-thirty."

"I would have called your private line but I don't have the number."

"Oh, damn. It's the main line. Hold on again." Another click.

While he waited he wondered about the timing of that maneuver. If she didn't want him to call, all she had to do was say so.

"Still there?"

"Hanging on your every word."

"I'll give you a word."

He smiled. "I see you're in a good mood."

"Yeah, terrific." She yawned into the phone and then murmured, "Sorry."

"Are you wearing that big ugly white bra?"

"What?"

"You know, the one you wore the other night. I miss it. I think it's my new fetish."

"You're a lunatic, you know that?" Sounded like she stifled another yawn. "So what's your other fetish?"

"Come over tonight and I'll show you."

Her silence gave him his answer.

"I talked to Dallas today," he said to ease the awkwardness.

"Me, too, but only briefly. I had to go to a meeting. Sounded like she's sold on cruising."

"Yeah, she's gonna be the next poster girl."

Another yawn.

"You sound exhausted. Can't you duck out early tonight? I still have some Chinese takeout here. That's it. Dinner and some quiet time. No ulterior motive. I promise."

"Tony, you can't keep tempting me like this."

He hesitated, not wanting to interfere. That hadn't been his intention. "You're right. Hey, I don't even like calling at work but it's the only number I have."

She snorted. "That's the only place you'd ever reach me."

He hadn't thought of that. It did make him feel marginally better. "Go ahead, get back to work. Sorry I interrupted."

"You didn't interrupt. I'm glad you called."

"Yeah, me, too," he said, taking the high road even though he sorely wanted to point out this should've been her call. "I'll talk to you some other time."

"Okay."

He was about to disconnect when he heard her.

"Tony, wait."

He brought the phone back to his ear. "I'm here."

"You're right. I am tired and not very productive. Want to meet at Samuel's Deli? It's after eight. Most of the dinner crowd should be gone."

"Fine." He knew the place, on a corner halfway between him and her flat. "An hour?"

She paused. "You say you still have Chinese?"

Tony smiled. The evening was looking up.

15

GOD, SHE WAS WEAK. Horribly, disgustingly weak. Yes, she was tired and leaving the office would make her more productive tomorrow morning. But only if she were going home. To bed. Alone. Not running to Tony.

They had to have a talk. She had to make him understand that time was her greatest ally and, yet, also her worst enemy. She had so damn little of it these days. In the end it would be worth it, but right now she had to pay her dues.

She'd knocked twice and when he hadn't answered, she'd started to think that maybe she'd gotten confused over where to meet. But then he opened the door, dressed in snug well-worn jeans, his hair damp, and looking as if he'd recently shaved. Looking as if he might be ready for the horizontal Olympics. Damn him.

He smiled, the warmth reaching his eyes, and stealing a piece of her heart. "Come in. It's freezing out there." Stepping aside, he rubbed his hands together and then quickly closed the door.

"Wow, you've really done a lot since I was here last." She looked around while he hung up her coat.

"The living room floor is new and you've done something to the mantle."

He nodded. "The upstairs guest bathroom has new tile and new countertops, too."

"How did you find the time?"

"First things first." He slid his arms around her from behind and pulled her against his chest. He kissed the back and side of her neck, soft leisurely kisses that gave her goose bumps, and then he slowly turned her around so that their lips met.

With his arms around her and her breasts pressed against his chest, the tension seemed to melt out of her. Disappear just like that. A dangerous illusion. Nothing changed. Tony couldn't change it.

She broke the kiss and reluctantly moved back. "I'm very jealous that you just had a shower."

"We can fix that. I'll even scrub your back."

"Oh, no." Laughing, she backed farther away. "We so can't go there."

"Okay, okay." He threw his hands up. "To the kitchen then."

She followed him, her gaze on his very fine backside, her pulse picking up speed. Why did she keep doing this to herself? She forced her gaze away and noticed the windows. "When did you put the blinds up?"

"About five minutes ago." He grinned, and she rolled her eyes at him. Nothing was going to happen tonight, if that's what he was thinking. She hoped. "I had to order custom because of the size. They were delivered this morning and I put them up while I was waiting for the bathroom grout to dry. Better than curtains, huh?"

"Definitely. The kitchen is modern and that plantation-style blind is perfect," she said, envy surprising her. As much as she'd love to have her own place to decorate, she doubted that would happen for a long while. She didn't have time or money. Certainly not for high-priced Manhattan real estate.

He got the cartons of Chinese food out of the fridge, taunting her with that perfect backside again. "I think I'll replace the living room drapes with the same thing."

She went for the plates, opening one wrong cabinet, then finding them on the second try. "I don't understand how you have time to do all this and still work." She turned and caught him checking out her legs. Fair was fair, she supposed.

He smiled. "This is my work."

"No, I was talking about your full-time job."

"This is it."

She didn't understand. "But you work for Capshaw Construction."

"Not anymore."

"When did you leave?"

"Right after Dallas quit."

"I didn't know…."

He chuckled. "Apparently not. You use chopsticks?"

She nodded numbly. No wonder he didn't understand how crunched she was for time. "I assumed you had a regular job."

He deposited the food in the microwave and started it. "I thought attorneys never assumed anything?"

She gave him a wry smile. "I'm curious. How do you sustain yourself?"

"When I'm done renovating, I sell."

"This one?" Disappointment welled up inside her. What did it matter? Probably better that he moved away. Back to Queens. Or Brooklyn. Or even the other side of Manhattan.

He studied her closely, close enough to make her uncomfortable and she turned away, busily gathering utensils and napkins.

"Why?"

She looked up and smiled. "It's really nice. You've done a wonderful job. I would think you'd hate to part with it."

"That's business," he said, shrugging. "I was hoping you were disappointed that I wouldn't be living so close."

The microwave buzzer went off, signaling the food was ready, but he stayed where he was, his gaze searching her face.

"Like we have a lot of time to see each other." She arched her brows in the direction of the microwave. "Are you going to get that?"

He blinked and looked away, but not before she saw the disappointment in his eyes. "Yeah."

She took a deep breath, getting ready for the plunge. "For me it's not going to get better, either. When Cody was trying to make partner he practically lived at the office. My father, too. When I was a kid, there were some weeks when the only time we saw him was at Sunday dinner."

"What about now?" he asked, totally expressionless as he carried the food to the table. "Does Cody have a life outside of the office? Does your dad?"

That stopped her. "Well, yes, of course," she said tentatively.

He didn't say anything, just pulled out their chairs.

"I mean, they attend all kinds of social events." She sat down, scooted her chair closer to the oak table and placed the napkin on her lap. "Dad's on several committees with the bar association—"

"You don't have to try and convince me." He swooped down and briefly kissed her before taking his seat.

"I'm not." Admittedly it sounded as if she were. "It's difficult to explain but when you love your work—"

"Hey, I guarantee you no one loves their work more than I do, but I still have a life."

She sighed, knowing this conversation would go nowhere. "Pass me the chow mein, please."

"Let's change the subject."

"Great idea."

"How about dinner Saturday night? Not here. I know this terrific restaurant in Soho—" He leaned back and frowned. "What?"

"I can't."

"You're working Saturday night?"

"I have a bar association dinner to go to. It's an annual thing that's not exactly mandatory, but absences are usually noticed." She'd had some trouble keeping the noodles on her chopsticks but she finally got them anchored. "Kind of a boring evening, especially since everyone takes their spouse or significant other."

At the expectant look on his face, she nearly dropped the chow mein, chopsticks and all. Did she have the biggest mouth on the planet, or what? She couldn't take him. He'd be bored silly. Most of the talk was legalese. It wouldn't be at all like chatting with the guys at Sargenttis. Prominent judges would be there. Hot-button legal issues discussed.

Chicken that she was, she shoved the noodles in her mouth so she wouldn't have to say anything more. She stared down at her food, hoping he hadn't seen in her eyes the ugliness that had gone through her head. That he might not fit in. That she would be uncomfortable.

"So even when you have a social life, it revolves around work?"

She kept chewing. The thought hadn't occurred to her, but yeah, pretty much. When she did go to a party, a colleague normally threw it. Her two friends from college both had busy careers and it seemed like every time they made dinner plans, one of them ended up canceling at the last minute.

"But that's pretty typical, really," she finally said after she thought about it. "Once we're out of school most of our social contacts evolve from work. If you go for a beer, I bet it's usually with the guys you used to work with."

He gave a small conciliatory nod. "Point taken. But at least it's my choice and I enjoy going."

She sighed. "Point taken."

He chuckled, and then sobered. "Don't go."

"To the association dinner? I have to."

"Why? You said it'll be boring."

"I also said that absences are noted."

"So what? You're a good lawyer. You have to be if you've been handed a high-profile case. Don't be bullied into rubbing elbows if you don't want to."

Sighing, she laid down her chopsticks. "It's not that simple, Tony."

She had to tell him. That's what she'd come here for. It should have been said already. Before too many other issues got in the way. But she'd kept her mouth shut for the same reason she was in trouble. He distracted her. With that sexy smile and those broad shoulders and strong arms of his, she got lost. Forgot that she didn't have the time to give to a relationship. Forgot that she had a goal, and frankly, he didn't fit into the plan.

She hadn't made the rules, but if she wanted to get ahead she had to damn well follow them. That part was very simple. And she'd known the drawbacks going in. She couldn't cry foul now.

And neither could he. All they'd ever shared was sex. No promises had been made. Not even implied. One day at a time. He'd said it himself.

"I forgot to get us something to drink." He got up. "Orange juice, water, wine or beer. Take your pick."

"Water is good." She watched him walk to the kitchen, his long legs taking slow, easy strides, and she thought about how she never walked slowly anymore. At work, she could be going to get a cup of coffee and she'd practically speed-walk to the lounge.

It seemed as if she was always running to a meeting or running to catch a cab or running to catch the elevator even, because God forbid she should wait five seconds for another one.

Only when she was with Tony did she slow down, savor every moment, every touch. Did she not think about work. Therein lay the problem.

"Here you go." He set a bottle of water beside her right hand and then leaned down for a kiss. His hand cupped her nape and he gently massaged her neck while he performed magic on her lips.

Her traitorous body immediately responded. Her nipples tightened and the flutter that started in her chest went down to her stomach and then settled between her thighs.

"You seriously need to relax," he said, continuing the seductive massage. "And I have just the thing."

"I can't have anything to drink. I have to get to the office early."

"What I have in mind won't give you a hangover. That's a promise."

He withdrew his hand from her neck and her entire body protested. She twisted around to look at him just as he reached for her hand. He pulled her to her feet and led her into the living room. She pretty much knew what he intended. What she didn't know was whether she had the willpower to stop him.

Did she want to? Would it be so bad to have this one more time with him? If this was a last time. It wasn't as if she could never see him again. It would just be a while before she had the time. And if all they wanted from each other was sex then...

She couldn't bear to finish the thought. To think their sole connection was based on sex stung. It simply wasn't true. In the beginning, yes, sex was all she wanted from him. But not now. Which made their relationship all the more difficult.

The thought shook her to her very core. When had it happened? When had she started caring? Wanting? Needing? Damn her. Damn Tony.

He sat her on the sofa, and then knelt down in front of her and slipped off one of her high heels.

"What are you doing?"

He slipped off the second heel, his chocolate-brown eyes sparkling when he looked up at her. "Reflexology."

"Right."

"You doubt me?"

She chuckled. "With all my heart."

"Smart woman."

He stared at her knees for a moment, looking confused, and then he inched up her hem.

"May I help you?" she asked, trying to sound indignant, and trying not to laugh.

"No, I think I got it." He found her garters and started to roll down her stocking.

"Hey." She clamped her knees together. "What are you doing?"

"Trust me."

She made a face. He hadn't tried to take her

clothes off, which would have made more sense. "Is this the other fetish you were talking about?"

"No," he said, frowning thoughtfully. "But this is right up there on the happy scale."

"Come on," she said sternly, "what are you doing?"

"This." He reached up her skirt, between her legs and found his target.

She gasped, stiffening, trying to squeeze her legs together. "Tony, we can't."

"*We* aren't doing anything. You just relax." He pushed the hem of her skirt up as far as he could, which ended up at midthigh, and then he smiled wryly, murmuring, "Plan B."

"Tony." She put a restraining hand on his shoulder. "Please."

"What are you going to do?"

"Can you trust me?"

She moistened her dry lips and nodded.

He kissed her while sliding his hands around her waist and finding the zipper to her skirt. She held her breath while he unhooked and unzipped and then pulled down her waistband as far as it would go. He tapped the side of her hip and she raised her bottom a little. Enough that he easily slid her skirt off, and then carefully folded it in two and laid it beside her on the sofa.

She sat there in bikini panties, one stocking, a lone black garter and her conservative white blouse. The panties Dallas had packed for her that fateful day, and only because Dakota hadn't done laundry in nearly two weeks.

Tony noticed and smiled. But didn't say anything, only got rid of her other stocking, again carefully, setting it atop her skirt. That he was going so damn slow did not help her to relax. Tension mounted with each careful movement even though she pretty much knew what he was going to do.

The anticipation, of course, was killing her. So was the fact that she couldn't touch him. Really touch him, not just clutch his shoulder or push her fingers through his hair when he got close enough.

He ran his palms down the outside of her thighs and she shivered in the warm house in front of the crackling fire. "By the way, honey, I know you weren't drunk."

Her sleepy eyes suddenly widened. "What do you mean?"

"The night of Dallas's wedding. When we flew to Bermuda. You weren't drunk. A little tipsy, I grant you." He kissed the inside of her knee. "You were pretending."

"Why would I do that?"

"Because you didn't know how to ask for what you want, or how to just take it."

"That's absurd." She tried to bring her knees together but he stopped her with a kiss higher up her thigh, inside, on the fleshy sensitive side. And she realized she might have made another faulty assumption about his intentions.

"And now?" He looked up into her eyes, his dark and glassy with a desire she knew well. He wasn't trying to humiliate her. Only trying to make a point. "All you have to do is ask."

She swallowed hard. Briefly closed her eyes. Heat tunneling through her, her entire body alive and waiting, down to the last strand of her hair. "Tony," she whispered, pleaded.

That was enough. He pulled off her panties, spread her thighs farther apart and kissed his way to a spot that made her squirm. Reaching his hands behind her, he pulled her hips toward him, and then his mouth was on her, his tongue delving, tasting, exploring. Plundering.

Reflexively, she tried to wriggle away, even though she didn't want him to stop. He used his fingers to spread her farther and with his persistent tongue found the little nub that made her scream. She put a hand over her mouth, her teeth biting into her palm as he brought her to the brink, and then slowly let her slip away.

Before she could protest, the assault resumed, fiercer, more relentless until she came so hard, so completely her entire body trembled violently. Her hand slipped from her mouth to fist his hair and her cry filled the room.

She started to retreat and Tony slowed his pace, finally bringing his head up to look at her, his eyes glazed and his lips damp. From her.

"I made a lot of noise," she said, her breathing so ragged she barely recognized her own voice.

He smiled and nodded.

"I hope your neighbors don't call the police."

"Let them." He kissed one thigh and then the other. "My attorney is present."

She laughed nervously, taking several deep breaths, trying to restore order, and arranging her blouse so she didn't feel so exposed. "Oh, yeah, that would be great."

He got up from his crouched position, and joined her on the couch, sliding an arm around her shoulders. He drew her close and kissed the top of her head. "Wasn't hard, was it? All you had to do was ask."

She moved her hand to his lap, and he stopped her from reaching his bulging fly. "Tony?"

He squeezed her hand. "Not this time."

She yawned. "I thought all I had to do was ask?"

Chuckling, he put his other arm around her so that she leaned against his chest, safe and warm, in the circle of his arms. "Rest," he whispered against her hair.

She couldn't. Not because she needed to go home, which she did, but because she hadn't accomplished what she'd come here to do. And now it would be horribly awkward.

"Would you hand me my skirt, please?" she asked, pulling away and avoiding his gaze.

Her tone came out formal and polite, which she totally hadn't meant. He apparently noticed, judging by the wariness in his eyes. He delivered the carefully folded skirt and stockings, and then kept his hands to himself as she searched the floor for her panties and then pulled them on.

Still sitting, she stepped into her skirt and pulled it up as far as it would go before she stood and finished the job. After she was zipped up, her blouse neatly tucked in and her stockings securely fastened by the garters, she looked over at him.

"Not even gonna stay for a cigarette?" Despite the wry smile and the teasing words, he knew. She saw it in his eyes.

She cleared her throat, and then lowered herself back to the sofa but kept close to the edge. "This is going to be a little awkward."

He sat patiently, waiting, totally expressionless, not giving her a bit of help.

"I didn't plan tonight to go like this." She briefly looked away to maintain her composure. "I wanted to have a nice quiet dinner and to talk."

"About?" His lips curved in a slow smile and she couldn't tell whether it was sad or strained from anger.

"Us. About how often we see each other." She paused, but he didn't react, just sat there. Annoying, but she had only herself to blame. "I'm under a lot of pressure at work, Tony, with this case I'm working on. What's making it more difficult is that I'm distracted."

He said flatly. "You don't want to see me anymore."

"No, it's not that. I do. I just can't. For now."

He nodded slowly. "I see."

"You don't. I can tell." She started to reach for his hand but stopped. "You should be flattered," she said with a small laugh. "I *want* to be with you. Hence, the distraction."

"I don't wanna be flattered." He held her gaze. "I want you."

Abruptly, she stood. "I can't afford a relationship right now."

"With me." His expression tightened.

"With anyone."

She moved away from the sofa, and he got up and went to the closet for her coat and jacket.

"Tony, please try to understand," she said as he helped her on with them.

Gently he fixed her collar. "I do." He smiled. "Don't let the bastards win again, Dakota." He kissed her on the cheek and then opened the door.

16

BRUCE WALKED INTO her office, his coat hooked on his thumb and slung over his shoulder. "A bunch of us are going over to Sargenttis if you want to—"

She briefly looked up. "No, thanks."

"If you change your mind, we'll be—"

"Have fun." She rudely cut him off, this time not looking up from the brief she was working on.

Damn it.

Sargenttis reminded her of Tony. She shoved the image of him from her mind. Two days since she'd seen him and she could still taste the finality of his last kiss. She couldn't think about it.

"See you tomorrow," Bruce muttered irritably and left.

She glanced at her watch. Six-forty-five. She'd be lucky if she made it home by midnight.

SARA KNOCKED and then entered Dakota's office before she was invited. Normally Dakota wouldn't mind. Today she gritted her teeth.

"I brought you a salad from that new—"

"I told you not to bring me any lunch." Dakota put

down her pen and rubbed her right temple. The headache that had started at seven this morning wouldn't quit. Not even after six aspirins.

"I know, but there's this new Italian deli that just opened and it's after two and you haven't eaten. In fact, you haven't been—"

"Sara?"

"Yes." She shrunk back a step, alarm in her blue eyes.

Italian deli. Hell, was everyone purposely trying to torture her? Four days since she'd seen Tony. He was probably making lasagna for someone else by now. The idea burned a hole in her stomach.

"I know you're well-intentioned," she told Sara as calmly as she could. "But don't you have some filing to do?"

Sara nodded and backed out of the office.

Dakota sighed, annoyed with herself. Sara was the last person she should be annoyed with. She was a great assistant, and a nice, caring person.

Damn that Tony.

"Do you have a minute?"

Dakota looked up at her brother standing at the door of her office. "No," she said, and went back to reviewing the new motion she'd received an hour ago. One week and counting since she'd seen Tony. Withdrawal was hell.

"Dakota?"

"I'm busy, Cody. Later."

Sara showed up alongside him, her eyes worried.

Probably thinking Dakota would get fired talking to one of her bosses that way. "May I get you anything? Coffee? Lunch?"

"Yes, as a matter of fact." She smiled sweetly, and looked at Cody. "His head on a platter if he doesn't get out of here in two seconds." Dismissively, she looked down at the motion. "And close the door behind you."

He ignored her, waved for Sara to leave and entered the lion's den. "What's going on, Dakota?"

"Nothing." God, she wished he'd leave. If he didn't she feared she'd say something she'd regret. Like quit being a damn coward and using pretend visits to her in order to see Sara. But she was hardly the person to call anyone else a coward.

"This isn't like you. You've been snapping at everyone who crosses your path for the past week. Poor Sara's even afraid to come in here."

Oh, God, but he was tempting her....

"I think maybe the pressure of this case is getting to you. Maybe I was wrong in naming you cocounsel."

She brought her head up. "Don't you dare."

His eyes were full of concern. "I didn't say I was going to pull you off the case." But he'd thought about doing so. It was written all over his face. "I'm thinking you could use more help."

"No." She shook her head. She knew how that went. Another attorney would be assigned to help her. After a couple of weeks, it would be simple to ease her out. But she'd given up too much already. She's sacrificed a chance with Tony. She couldn't let Cody take this opportunity away from her. "I know

I've been irritable. I apologize. Something personal came up. But I've taken care of it."

He stayed where he was, silently assessing her. She wanted him to speak or leave, but now wasn't the time to bite his head off. So she waited.

"Tony?" he finally asked.

"How would that concern you?"

"I know you haven't been seeing him. You're always the first here, and the last to leave."

"This is so not like you to get personal. Don't start now."

He smiled. "You've been putting in too many hours. It's taking its toll. Take a rest, Dakota."

She stared in disbelief. He looked like her brother. Must be an illusion.

He got to the door, paused and hit his palm against the door frame. "For God's sake, go see him," Cody said and then left without a glance.

Dakota sank back in her chair. Was Mercury in retrograde? Was everyone going crazy? She stared at her phone. It wouldn't hurt to at least call him. Would it?

TONY HAD TO GET to the market soon. One more peanut butter and jelly sandwich and he'd croak. Even Chinese food had gotten old. He'd have to start getting to know the neighborhood and pick up a few takeout menus. Better yet, find the places that delivered.

He didn't like going out if he could help it. Commuting to the coffeepot was as far as he'd gone the past week. Maybe this weekend he'd take his mother up on dinner. She always made a ton of food, which meant she'd send him home with a care package that would keep him fed for three days.

She'd called and asked him to come over twice, and both times he'd made an excuse. Then his sister had called and started bugging him. It was as if they had some kind of radar that told them when he was in a rotten mood and wanted to hide. Could they respect that? Of course not. They had to nag. He loved his family but...

His cell rang again and he pulled it off his belt, prepared to turn the thing off and let voice mail pick up the message. But he saw that it was Dallas and hesitated. He wasn't sure he even wanted to talk to her—the subject of Dakota would come up.

It rang the final time before she would be sent to voice mail.

Shit.

He gave in. "Hi."

"Hey, Tony. It's me. Busy?"

"I just finished a peanut butter and jelly sandwich. What does that tell you?"

"That if you keep eating those you're going to end up weighing a ton."

"That'll be the day." He wiped the counter and put the peanut butter away as he talked.

"How's the house coming?"

"Ahead of schedule. Sylvia already has a buyer."

"Oh." Dallas sighed. "I was hoping you'd keep that one. It's nice having you live in Manhattan."

He snorted to himself. He'd thought so once. "Are you back at work?"

"Oh, yeah. In fact, I only have a minute, but I wanted

to see if you and Dakota want to come over for dinner and look at our honeymoon pictures this weekend?"

He sat down. "Have you talked to her?"

"Not for the past week. I left a message yesterday but she hasn't called me back yet."

"She has a bar association dinner on Saturday." He didn't want to get into it with Dallas about her sister. At least he hadn't lied.

"Oh yeah, I forgot that was coming up this weekend. Are you going with her?"

"No. Look I have another call I've been expecting. I've gotta go."

"Me, too. Call me later."

He disconnected, feeling so miserable and confused he wanted to punch a wall. He missed Dakota, but he couldn't abide by her terms. He couldn't see her exhausted, and be stretched every which way.

And truthfully, he didn't know where he stood with her. He didn't have a comparable education and he didn't wear a suit to work every day. Was that a problem for her? Did she feel that he reflected negatively on her and her career? Is that why she hadn't asked him to go to the dinner? He wasn't sure. But if that was true, he sure as hell wouldn't roll over for that kind of thing. She had a lot to figure out.

The phone rang again, and when he checked, he was surprised to see that it was Dakota. Smiling sadly, he turned it off.

DAKOTA SIPPED her first cup of morning coffee, wondering if she should try calling Tony again. He always had his phone on him, and it wasn't like him to not answer. Unless he was avoiding her. The thought stabbed at her but what did she expect? She was the one who'd told him she didn't have time for a relationship. Maybe it was for the best that he hadn't returned either of her calls. What did she really have to say to him that would change things?

Like every other morning this week, she'd arrived at the office first. Not to get a head start, but to catch up from the day before. Yes, admittedly she'd been distracted by Tony, but that wasn't the only thing hindering her productivity. She hated the case she was working on. She despised the client and thought the smug bastard was as guilty as the devil himself.

Cody had warned her about letting her bias show. Reminded her she wasn't a judge yet. That had royally ticked her off. But her brother had a habit of doing that, anyway. To think she'd agreed to go with him to the bar association dinner.

Just thinking about Saturday night knotted her stomach. The dinner itself wasn't the problem. But it reminded her of the look on Tony's face when she'd brought it up. He'd obviously expected her to ask him to go, but she hadn't, and he'd done the math.

But he had part of the equation wrong. He didn't embarrass her. In the beginning she'd feared judgment and talk because he didn't fit in with her circle of friends and colleagues. What a joke. What friends? Her two law school pals were just as busy as she was and their plans to see one another never happened. If anything, she embarrassed herself, for the kind of person she'd become. So like the peers she privately criticized.

And now she was about to blow one of the best things that had ever happened to her. Sadly, she didn't even know what to do about it. Her workload wouldn't change. She didn't have time to spare. How could she ask him to accept crumbs? How could she go back to her drab life?

She needed to talk to someone before she went crazy. Dallas. Dakota owed her a call anyway. She checked her watch. Only seven-ten. If she called this early, Dallas would bite her head off.

There was always the Eve's Apple gang. Someone might be online, or have posted a bit of wisdom for her to hang on to. Like a junkie looking for a fix, she couldn't get her laptop on her desk and operational fast enough. As she signed on she realized how important the group had become to her. Most of the time she dismissed the advice, often laughed at some of their theatrics, but once in a while, just at the right time, she'd read a thought-provoking post that hit so close to home it lingered for days.

She decided to read first and then possibly post, for cathartic reasons if nothing else. The anonymity of the group allowed her to speak freely and she hadn't appreciated the opportunity as much as she did right now.

A lot of new activity had popped up since she'd last checked in and she scanned the older posts first, some chatty, some more serious stuff, the camaraderie already making her feel better. She read a general posting from Color Me Happy about a reunion with a high school boyfriend after being apart for eight years. Then she found one in response to one of her earlier posts.

To: LegallyNuts@EvesApple.com
From: Colorado Jane@EvesApple.com
Subject: Check out his wallet
D,
Hey, girlfriend, take some advice from a single fellow lawyer also looking to get laid. Make sure the guy has some dough of his own. Yeah, I like the more brawn than brains type, too, who isn't afraid of getting down and dirty. But I've had two different but equally bad experiences with the type. Either they think you're their meal ticket. You know, sit at home and drink beer while you bust your ass at the office. Or the other scenario is the damn Neanderthal gets it in his thick head that you've undermined his manhood because you make more money than him. Either way it sucks. The sex stinks after that and there's no going back. So, girlfriend, I urge you, make him show you the money.
Wishing you luck in this crazy singles' world.
Jane

Tony wasn't like that. He'd never be so petty or sexist. He was far too secure and comfortable in his own skin. That was one of the qualities she liked best about him. Besides, money seemed to be the least of his interests. Jane from Colorado meant well but she was so off base.

Dakota's ridiculous annoyance stopped her. She felt like a mother lion protecting her cub. What was she doing taking this stranger's words as a personal affront to Tony?

She calmed down, reminding herself that Jane was venting. Her e-mail actually had little to do with Dakota or anything she'd posted. In fact, Dakota hadn't revealed anything too specific…. She hoped.

Uneasiness had her thinking back on her e-mails. How much had she mentioned about Tony? She'd been careful, remaining vague, except, admittedly, a couple of nights ago she'd been so down and miserable she never should have gotten on the computer. Had she said too much?

It didn't matter. No one knew who she was. She hadn't even used her name. Just her first initial. She scrolled down and one of the subject lines caught her eye.

To: The Gang at Eve's Apple
From: JustSara@EvesApple.com
Subject: Lonely and the City
Hi, y'all,
Thought I'd check in. It's Thursday night. Nothing to do, as usual. I'm all alone in my apartment, except for the little lost kitty who showed up at my door. She's so cute and I like the company. Maybe tomorrow night I'll venture out again and try to meet new people. I'd rather be venturing out with you-know-who from the office but I'm starting to lose faith. Sometimes I think he's interested and

other times, I swear, he treats me like something he picked up on his shoe.

Anyway, I refuse to fret over him. If he's not interested enough to get to know me, well then, I guess it's his big fat loss.

Boy, I sounded brave, didn't I? :) I owe it all to y'all. One of these days I'm gonna have Mr. Big Shot Attorney on his knees begging. You wait and see.

I'll check in tomorrow. Hope y'all are having a good night.

Bye for now,
Sara

Dakota stared at the screen. Reread the moniker and then the sign-off, her pulse doing double time. It couldn't be. Oh, God, not her Sara. How awful would that be? Why hadn't Dakota noticed her posts before now? As if she weren't too self-absorbed. Getting upset was ridiculous. Sara was a common name, and she hadn't said anything about living in New York City. But Mr. Big Shot Attorney? The y'alls? Oh, God. It sure sounded like Sara. And if it was, and she'd read any of Dakota's posts and knew it was her, she'd just die.

She quickly got offline and turned off the computer as if someone from Eve's Apple could actually see her. That was it. No more going there. Except to read posts. Maybe figure out if that was *the* Sara.

So much for that. She drummed her fingers on the desk and stared at the clock. Dallas wasn't exactly a morning person, and she normally didn't go to her office until later. But Eric had to be up by now.

Dakota couldn't stand it. She picked up the receiver and pressed the speed dial number, taking deep breaths while the phone rang.

"Is it too early?"

"Dakota?" Dallas sounded as if she might have been asleep. "What's going on?"

"I can call back later," she said reluctantly.

"No, no, I'm awake. I just haven't had my first cup of coffee yet. Are you okay?"

"Oh, yeah, I'm fine." Dakota sighed. "Relatively speaking."

"Uh-oh. Is this about work or Tony?"

Dakota hesitated. What the hell was she thinking? Did she really want to get her sister involved? But if not Dallas, whom else could she talk to? "Tony," she said quietly, the admission feeling like a lead weight on her tongue. "Have you talked to him?"

"Yesterday. What happened?"

"Did he say anything?"

"About you?" Dallas paused, and Dakota could hear her taking a sip of coffee. "Not really. I asked him if you guys wanted to come over for dinner tomorrow night and he reminded me that you had the bar association dinner. That's about it."

"Oh."

"So?"

"What?"

"So you didn't call me at seven-thirty in the morning just to ask if I spoke to Tony."

Dakota cleared her throat. "No, I, um, I'm not sure why I called to be honest." She wasn't lying. If Tony had said something then that would have opened the conversation. But he hadn't said a word, probably because he hadn't given her another thought.

"I figured you wanted my opinion as to whether you should ask him to go to the dinner."

"No," she said a little too quickly. "I mean how boring would that be."

Dallas laughed. "Tony is never bored. In fact, if the dinner gets too boring, he'll liven things up."

Dakota didn't say anything.

"Are you afraid he'd embarrass you?" Dallas asked slowly.

"Of course not. It's just that Cody and Dad and my boss and, well you know, everyone will be there." Meaning those who could influence her career. She briefly closed her eyes. "Oh, God, Dallas, please tell me I'm not getting to be like Cody."

"You've got a ways to go yet." Dallas laughed softly. "But I'd hate to see you head in that direction."

Cody's world revolved around his career. Everything he owned or did somehow enhanced his position in the firm or legal community. Is that how Dakota wanted to end up? Was being a judge so important to her that the journey should be sacrificed?

Don't let the bastards win again.

Tony's words haunted her.

She knew damn well what he'd meant. College. The dean. Her whole life she'd allowed other people to decide what was right for her. Her mother and father and Cody. But Tony was right. She was a damn good attorney. Her merit alone would have to be enough.

"Dakota?"

"What?"

"Don't snap at me. I wasn't the one who called you."

"Sorry." She looked at her watch. A cab was going to be tough to find soon with everyone trying to get to the office. "Look, Dallas, I have to go."

She had to talk to Tony. Before it was too late.

17

TONY POURED his fifth cup of coffee and then remembered his cell phone was still in the living room
where it had been charging since last night. He didn't
expect any calls. Most of them he wasn't answering
anyway. But on the off chance that the bathroom
wallpaper he'd ordered had arrived early, he'd been
checking for messages.

And shit, yeah, he wanted to know if Dakota had
called again. Ironically she'd finally left her direct line
number. But he just wasn't ready to call her. He was
still mad and hurt at being rejected. And since that had
nothing to do with her precious career, he doubted she
gave a rat's ass, so why put himself through it again?

One message. From his mother. She wanted to
know about dinner. Nothing from Dakota. Probably
got tired of him not returning her calls. Disappointment made his coffee taste bitter so he set his mug
on the end table, then sprawled out on the couch. The
good thing about leather was that it didn't matter if
his jeans and shirt were dusty as hell. He'd gotten up
earlier than usual, close to five, and immediately had
gone to work in the guest room.

With so much time on his hands, he'd made awesome progress in the past week. Sylvia was going to be happy. His neighbors most likely weren't. In fact, they'd probably throw a party when he left the neighborhood. Even though he tried to keep the pounding and drilling confined to midday.

The thought of leaving still didn't sit well. Not that it should matter where he lived if he weren't seeing Dakota. Besides, Sylvia had found him another town house on the east side for which he was about to sign a contract. It was a sweet deal and Sylvia already had two buyers who were interested.

God bless lazy rich people. Life had been pretty damn good lately. Only Dakota would make it better. He abruptly stood and grabbed his mug. Sneaky unwelcome thoughts like that really pissed him off. The woman had issues to resolve. Nothing to do with him. Nothing he could do about it.

On his way to the kitchen, the doorbell rang. He looked at his watch. Who the hell could that be at eight-forty? He wasn't expecting a delivery. He used the peephole. What the—?

Dakota stood with her arms wrapped around herself, without a coat, and shivering.

He took a deep breath and opened the door.

"Hi." She looked him up and down. "Glad I didn't wake you."

"Come in."

She gave him a tentative smile and walked past him. "Where's your coat?"

"I forgot it." She moistened her lips. "I was in

a hurry," she said, her voice breaking when her teeth chattered.

"But it's only in the thirties."

"Believe me, I know." She gave a shaky laugh, vigorously rubbing her arms.

"Come here." He didn't have to say another word. She walked into his arms and they stood quietly in the foyer as he warmed her. "Don't you have enough sense to come in out of the cold?" he whispered, enjoying the feel of her, the smell of her more than he should.

"That's why I'm here." She tilted her head back to look at him, her eyes searching his face, her words loaded with meaning. She had a smudge on her nose, probably from his T-shirt.

He moved back, glanced down at his dusty clothes, and then at her beige suit. He didn't want to think about what her words implied. Better not to read too much into them. "Look what I did."

She looked, ignored it, and smiled at him. "Will you come to the bar association dinner with me tomorrow night?"

Taken by surprise he reared his head back. "Tomorrow?"

She nodded.

"I'll have to check my calendar."

She blinked. "Okay."

"That was a joke."

"Oh."

He stared at her for a moment, wanting to pull her against him but knowing they had some talking to do. "Coffee?"

"Definitely." Rubbing her hands together, she followed him into the kitchen.

"About this dinner, your date cancel at the last minute, or something?"

She gave him a dry look. "No, I was going alone. If you don't count my brother and father."

"Ah, they'll be there, huh?"

She nodded, and immediately took a sip from the steaming mug he handed her.

"And it won't be a problem with me going?"

"Why would it?" She conveniently looked away to pull up a bar stool.

He smiled and poured himself more coffee. "Why?"

"Why what?"

"Why did you change your mind?"

She shrugged. "I—it wasn't that—" Her shoulders sagged. "I'm tired of forgetting my coat."

He laughed. "What?"

"I'm tired of not laughing. I'm tired of not having something to look forward to at the end of the day. And I definitely don't want to let the bastards win again."

Tony smiled.

"Most of all, I miss you." Her lips quivered. "With you I live life in color. Without you it's black and white." She shook her head. "I can't do black and white anymore."

He put his mug down. "I've missed you, too."

She tried to fake a pout but a smile tugged at her mouth. "So why didn't you return my calls?"

"Because I wanted you to figure out what you

wanted. If you thought I'd stand in the way of your career then I was willing to back off."

She opened her mouth to protest, but then said nothing and sheepishly looked down at her hands. "You're right. I'm embarrassed to admit that the thought had crossed my mind that you couldn't fit into my life." Her laugh was terse. "Then I realized I didn't even have one."

"It's okay."

"No, it's not. I was an ass."

"Look, I don't know where this is going," he said, tugging her toward him until she went into his arms. "But I'm on the bus. Wherever it takes us."

"Me, too." Sliding her arms around his waist, she sighed. "Do you know how long this past week has felt?"

He rested his chin on top of her head. "Oh, I have some idea." He smiled and inhaled the fresh herbal scent of her shampoo. "What did you mean about being tired of forgetting your coat?"

She moved back to look at him. "I was in such a tizzy all week I kept forgetting my coat, my purse, where I put my keys. I couldn't even concentrate on work. Basically, I was a mess."

"Ah, so you're just using me."

Grinning, she traced a finger down his fly. "Shamelessly."

"Better not start something you can't finish," he said, his jeans immediately starting to get snug.

"We should go away for a weekend again. To another island, or maybe someplace in Vermont where we could get snowed in for a week." She quickly added, "But this time I'm paying."

"I'm the old-fashioned type. That would hurt my feelings." He leaned in for a kiss but she resisted.

She looked seriously at him. "Would it bother you being with a woman who makes more money than you?"

"Nah, I could get used to it."

She obviously couldn't tell if he were joking or not, and it seemed important to her.

He stole a quick kiss, and then said, "While you're here, would you do me a favor?"

She seemed startled, but nodded. "Of course."

"I need some legal advice."

Her eyebrows rose. "Okay."

He went to the corner cabinet where he kept his paperwork and brought out the contract Sylvia had dropped off. "If you could look over this contract before I sign it…"

"You know I'm not a contract lawyer."

"Yeah, but you've got to be able to do a better job of reviewing this than I can."

"What sort of contract is it?"

"Real estate."

"You're selling this wonderful brownstone?"

"Nope. I'm buying another one."

She frowned. "Let's see."

He handed it to her and watched her face as she read over the document. Normally he wouldn't reveal personal information like this. In fact, no one but his attorney and accountant knew his financial status.

But since Dakota seemed hung up on the money issue he figured this was as good a way as any to let her know he could afford a lousy vacation.

She frowned again when she got to the terms of sale part. "Have you read this yet?"

"Pretty much. Great price, huh?"

"This says you're agreeing to pay cash."

"Yeah, I know. My accountant doesn't like it. Says I'm foolish and I should borrow, but I prefer to pay cash and then get a credit line for the renovation material. It's been working out great so far."

Her brows drew together in confusion. "How did you pay for this place?"

"Cash."

Her lips parted in surprise, and he really wanted to kiss her. He would later. "How many houses do you own?"

"Just this one right now. I don't like to juggle more than two at a time. Then I'd have to start hiring people and I like working by myself just fine."

"Wow!"

"So the contract looks okay?" he asked with a straight face.

"Um, yes, fine."

He took the papers from her and set them aside. Then he took each of her hands and put them on either side of his neck. "One more question," he said, while molding his palms to her hips. "It won't bother you going out with a guy who makes more money than you, will it?"

She pressed her lips together, wincing. "Ouch! I guess I deserved that."

"I'll give you something you deserve." He lowered his head and she met him halfway.

Their lips barely touched but his body had already ignited. Deepening the kiss, he pulled her close so she could feel his desire. She clutched his shoulders and moved against him, swaying and rubbing and awakening every primal instinct he possessed.

"Have a feeling you're gonna be late for work?" he whispered against her mouth.

"What work?"

He pushed off her jacket but he only got her out of one sleeve before she unbuckled his belt. Her nipples were hard and pressing through her bra against her white cotton blouse. He touched one, circling it with his forefinger, and she whimpered softly.

"Want to try another room?" he asked. "Lots of blinds and curtains."

"Hmm, how about the bedroom for a change?"

He smiled. "What a novel idea."

Epilogue

One year later

TONY COULD HEAR the San Angelo clan laughing from clear across the large banquet room. Cousins he hadn't seen in years were here. His great aunt Francesca had come all the way from Rome to see him get married. He was glad to see her.

He stared at Dakota, sitting beside him, looking extraordinarily beautiful in her cream-colored silk dress. "Quite a diverse group we have here, huh?"

"Gee, you noticed."

They both laughed. On the right were the San Angelos, talking, laughing, dancing and sampling the hors d'oeuvres with gusto. On the left were the Sheas' friends and colleagues, looking shell-shocked. They probably still hadn't gotten over the amount of rice that had been dumped outside the small Manhattan church where he'd promised to love and cherish Dakota just a short hour ago.

Like he needed a piece of paper or preacher to tell him to do that. He looked at his new wife, emotion swelling in his chest. God, but how he loved this woman. Smart, gorgeous, kind and the best friend he'd ever had.

By mutual agreement, the ceremony had been simple. No attendants in tuxedos or fancy dresses. The exchange of vows had been kept short. The party, however, they'd gone all out for. With an equal amount of diplomacy and firmness they'd managed to maintain control of the event.

Instead of a formal sit-down dinner, they had food stations set up in each corner serving ethnic finger food. Every form of liquor was available from two very busy bars. His sister and Dallas had handled the decorations and flowers, which turned out tasteful enough to even meet his new mother-in-law's approval.

"This doesn't seem real, does it?" Dakota said softly and laid her head on his shoulder.

"Tired?"

"Exhausted."

"Exactly what we were trying to avoid by having a small wedding."

She brought her head up to smile at him. "But then we invited half of New York to the party."

"Yeah, well, we're only doing this once."

"You better believe it." She leaned in for a brief kiss, then her lips curved in a mischievous smile. "If you're a good boy, you might get lucky tonight."

"I'm always good. Ask any of the ladies."

"Why do I put up with you?"

"I can think of one big reason."

She rolled her eyes. "Oh, brother."

"Speaking of whom." Tony motioned with his chin toward the door where Cody had just arrived. "Did you notice my proper use of *whom?*"

"I did."

Someone got in the way and Dakota craned her neck to keep sight of Cody. Her hair was down and she'd done something to make it slightly curly. She looked beautiful. But of course she always did. Especially when she first woke up in the morning.

"Okay, now watch. I'm not wrong about this."

Tony sighed. "You and Dallas should go into business together. Matchmakers, Inc."

She gave him one of her stern lawyerly looks. "Are you complaining?"

"No, ma'am."

"Anyway, I'm not matchmaking. Sara isn't right for him, and she told me yesterday she's going back to Atlanta. I'm simply observing. In fact, I'll bet you that he makes contact within…" She checked her watch. "Five minutes. Are we on?"

"What's the bet?" He checked his watch, too.

"You don't trust me?"

"Why would I? You're a lawyer."

"Say that louder." Dakota gave him a cheeky look and turned back toward Cody. "Aha!"

Curious himself, Tony spied Cody talking to Sara. "Well, whaddya know. He's smiling. First time, huh?"

"Hey, that's my brother you're talking about." She grinned. "But I think you're right."

She also had the best smile. The best eyes. The best hair. The best heart. She was everything any man could possibly hope for.

And she was all his.

And he was hers.

Forever.

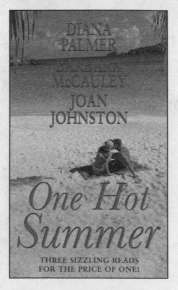

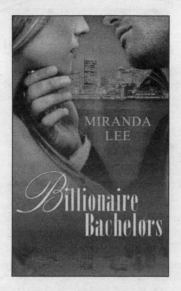

FREE!

2 Books
and a surprise gift!

We would like to take this opportunity to thank you for reading this Mills & Boon® book by offering you the chance to take TWO more specially selected titles from the Blaze® series absolutely FREE! We're also making this offer to introduce you to the benefits of the Mills & Boon® Reader Service™—

- ★ **FREE home delivery**
- ★ **FREE gifts and competitions**
- ★ **FREE monthly Newsletter**
- ★ **Exclusive Reader Service offers**
- ★ **Books available before they're in the shops**

Accepting these FREE books and gift places you under no obligation to buy, you may cancel at any time, even after receiving your free shipment. Simply complete your details below and return the entire page to the address below. You don't even need a stamp!

YES! Please send me 2 free Blaze books and a surprise gift. I understand that unless you hear from me, I will receive 4 superb new titles every month for just £3.10 each, postage and packing free. I am under no obligation to purchase any books and may cancel my subscription at any time. The free books and gift will be mine to keep in any case.

K7ZEF

Ms/Mrs/Miss/Mr ....Initials ....

BLOCK CAPITALS PLEASE

Surname ....

Address ....

....

....Postcode ....

Send this whole page to:
UK: FREEPOST CN81, Croydon, CR9 3WZ